Hidden by magic...
but for how long?

Randal moved quickly into the inner room and gestured at the stranger to follow him. Once they were both inside, Randal closed the door after them—and not a moment too soon. Footsteps sounded in the outer room. Someone was coming. The young wizard and the man he had rescued flattened themselves against the wall.

Quickly, Randal cast the spell of invisibility over himself and his companion. A second later a pale blue light showed around the edge of the door as it opened. Carvelli came in, a magical cold-flame glowing above one upraised hand. *So Carvelli is the magician,* thought Randal, *but not trained at the School of Wizardry. If we're in luck, he won't detect us.*

Carvelli drew a dagger from his belt with his left hand, while he pulled a sword with his right. "Whoever is here," he said slowly, "show yourselves now."

DANGER IN THE PALACE

Originally published as
Circle of Magic: Danger in the Palace

Debra Doyle and James D. Macdonald

illustrated by Judith Mitchell

SCHOLASTIC INC.

New York Toronto London Auckland Sydney
Mexico City New Delhi Hong Kong Buenos Aires

ISBN 0-439-70365-4

12 11 10 9 8 7 6 5 4 3 2 1   4 5 6 7 8 9/0

Printed in the U.S.A.   40

First Scholastic printing, December 2004

For Bruce Coville,
who provided encouragement and example,
and who beat some sense into our heads

I.

Market Square Magician

"A PENNY, a penny for art!"

Randal gave his cry again and showed the crowd an empty hat. The small cap of green felt belonged to Lys, his friend and traveling companion. The black-haired girl in boy's clothing sat on the rim of the enormous bronze-and-marble fountain in the center of Peda's market square, ready to begin her performance. Randal flourished the hat a second time and placed it on the ground. Then he sat cross-legged on the pavement and waited for Lys to start singing.

Behind him, the first notes of the girl's song floated out over the sound of falling water. Most of the people in the small crowd turned their attention to her. Those who still looked at Randal saw a tall, sturdily built youth in his middle teens, with untrimmed brown hair falling down into his eyes. Over his travel-stained garments he wore the wide-sleeved black robe of a journeyman wizard trained at the Schola Sorceriae—the School of Wizardry in Tarnsberg, on the western sea.

Time to start earning my bread, he thought, as Lys sang on. He didn't understand the words of her song—they were in her native Occitanian, the language of these parts, and Randal knew little more of that tongue than the few memorized phrases he'd already spoken. But he and Lys had practiced this routine every day on the road south from Widsegard; he knew the exact moment at which to begin weaving his own spells into the music.

Now the young wizard calmed his mind and began to call forth sound from the air around him— a deep-pitched, steady chord to underlie and harmonize with Lys's melody.

The chord came in well-balanced and firm on the first try. *Good,* thought Randal. *Now for the high tone.* He concentrated again and set a mellow flutelike tone playing along an octave above the tune Lys sang.

The flute sound also came in on key and followed the melody without any fumbles or mistakes. Randal allowed himself a smile of satisfaction—the music was going well today. *Now for the lights.*

He tried for a glowing cloud of color, like a veil between Lys and the spray of the fountain, and it appeared. With a little more concentration, he gave the cloud a wash of red for the low note of his chord, mingled with green and blue for Lys's clear alto voice and dappled with flecks of gold sparkling in time with the highest notes of the flute.

The first magic Randal had ever seen had been just such a display of sound and light. But Madoc the Wayfarer, the wizard who had performed those wonders in the great hall of Castle Doun, had been a master of the magical art and not a mere journeyman. Randal himself had spent the past few months in acquiring, by trial and error, the fine control that produced a particular sound or color without accident every time.

Some days the magic had worked well, while on other days Randal's efforts had brought him more embarrassment than success. But as traveling entertainers went, he and Lys had prospered— they'd always had enough money to buy food, and here in the southland, where nights were warm and dry, they slept in the open and seldom needed to pay for lodging.

As Lys's song came to an end, Randal ended the sounds and the cloud of colored light. He looked down at the cap and found it empty.

I don't understand, he thought, feeling at once puzzled and disappointed. *I've had the spells working right for weeks now, and Lys doesn't even need magic to sound good. We should have gotten one or two pennies at least from this crowd.*

Instead, only thin applause came from the small—and rapidly dwindling—audience. Randal sighed and reached out to pick up the empty cap. His fingers had just touched the brim when a small bag of black velvet sailed through the air and landed in the cap with a metallic *chink.*

Randal picked up the bag. It felt heavy in his hand, and the contents shifted and clinked inside it. Carefully he undid the silver cord of the drawstring and pulled the bag open. His sudden hopes were not dashed. The bag contained gold coins—more money than he'd seen in one place since leaving his uncle's castle to study wizardry.

Randal closed the bag and slid it into the deep pocket of his robe, next to his spell-book. Then he looked to see who had made the donation. The young wizard's gaze traveled upward from a man's high leather boots, to a short tunic of black velvet trimmed in silver, to a clean-shaven, intelligent face framed by bright red hair. At his waist, the stranger wore a long, narrow-bladed sword.

"Many thanks, my lord," said Randal in Occitanian, thus exhausting his entire stock of the language.

The well-dressed stranger gestured at Randal to rise and said something in a clear, pleasant voice. Randal looked around to Lys for a translation.

The Occitanian girl swung down from the rim of the fountain onto the pavement. Randal saw that her eyes were dancing. "Come on, Randy," she said. "We're going with this gentleman. He wants us to play at the palace."

"The palace?" Randal said in amazement as they fell in behind the stranger. "I knew we were good, but I didn't think we were that good."

"Here in Occitania," said Lys, "every city is its own country—and the lords of the city-states are rich and powerful. Just take what you can and smile. At the very least we can expect a good meal, and maybe even new clothes, when we play for His Grace."

Randal nodded, still uncertain whether the sum-

mons was for good or ill. Lys, though, seemed to have no doubts at all; she was smiling as they followed the stranger away from the marketplace. The red-headed man led them through the town and uphill along wide streets, through ranks of tall stone houses. At the top of the hill they came to a huge marble building—actually a collection of buildings joined together by walls and set in the midst of green lawns and sweet-smelling gardens.

Randal and Lys followed their guide onward through a maze of corridors, cloisters, enclosed gardens, and winding stairways. Everywhere they looked, they saw luxury. Frescoes covered the walls and the ceiling; dark and light woods made patterns on the polished floor underfoot; and bronze and marble statues filled the corners along the way.

This has to be the palace, thought Randal, feeling shabby and insignificant in his mud-stained robe. *No one but a prince would live in such magnificence.*

At last the three of them came to a small room where another man waited. The two strangers spoke together, and then the red-headed man said something to Randal.

"He wants you to go with him," Lys translated. "I'm supposed to stay here."

"Do I have any choice?" Randal asked.

"No," said Lys. "He's the Prince's messenger— you'd better go with him."

Randal followed the red-headed man down another series of corridors to a room filled with books. The messenger stopped, turned to Randal, and spoke a short phrase. Randal guessed that it meant something like "stay here"; he nodded, bowed, and clasped his hands before him in a gesture of patience. The response appeared to satisfy the messenger. He departed through another door, leaving Randal behind to look around curiously.

One side of the long, narrow room was all windows, opening onto a walled garden. Bookshelves lined the other walls from floor to ceiling. The sight of the rows of books carried Randal back for a moment to his early days at the Schola. *The library in Tarnsberg,* he remembered with a smile, *was the first one I'd ever seen.*

If truth be told, in those days he'd barely been able to read. In kingless, unsettled Brecelande, where he'd been born, knowledge of letters had mattered less than skill with a sword. But Randal had given up his future as heir to a northern barony to study the art of magic and had forsworn the use of knightly weapons forever. Now the fat, leather-bound volumes seemed to call to him from the library walls.

He contented himself, however, with scanning the titles of the ones nearest to him. The names intrigued him, and he was debating with himself the wisdom of taking down a book when he heard the sound of the far door opening. The red-headed man beckoned to him from the doorway. Randal left the bookshelves and went past the messenger into the next room.

The door closed behind him. Suddenly, the air was filled with the intense, neck-prickling sensation of powerful magic. Randal felt other, non-material locks and barriers slip into place.

Is this a trap? he thought, fighting a surge of panic. But when no immediate dangers arose to menace him, he forced himself to look calmly around the chamber. The books and equipment scattered about only confirmed what he had already guessed—he was in the workroom of a master wizard.

The dark, hawk-nosed man waiting at the desk, then, must be the wizard to whom the room belonged. To Randal, he seemed richly enough dressed to be the Prince himself. His long robe was cloth-of-gold, embroidered over with mystic signs in silver and black, and the ankle-length tunic beneath it was made of crimson silk. He waved away the messenger, then gestured at Randal to come forward.

"Come here," he said. "I want to look at you."

Randal obeyed. The dark man had spoken in the Old Tongue, the common language of wizards and wizardry. Now the man placed the tips of his long fingers together and regarded Randal with a penetrating gaze.

"Are you aware," the dark man continued, "that here in Peda all magic is the property of the Prince? And that I am the only wizard whom His Grace sees fit to let practice the Art?" He paused. "And are you aware of the penalties for violating His Grace's will?"

Randal felt cold. *Lys never warned me about anything like this,* he thought. *It wasn't enough that I got myself and Nick thrown into jail back in Widsegard, just for* looking *like I might be a wizard.*

The memory hurt. Nicolas Wariner had been the

first friend Randal had made among the apprentices at the Schola, and Nick had died by magic in Widsegard—died while aiding Randal to fight off the attack of an outlaw wizard. *If I hadn't asked for help, Nick would be alive today.*

For a moment Randal's guilt threatened to overwhelm him, as it had so many times since then, but he forced himself to push it aside. At least the pain of remembering had helped him in one way, by driving out the fear that the Prince's wizard had aroused. "No, Master," he said aloud. "I wasn't aware of the laws in Peda. I only arrived here a day ago."

The master wizard nodded. "You gave your first performance in the market square yesterday evening, and by this morning I had heard the news." He leaned back in his chair, and his voice took on a more kindly tone. "Fortunately, Prince Vespian the Magnificent, the Prince of Peda, gives me much freedom of action in magical matters. Therefore, I ask you—amaze me."

It sounded more like an order than a request. Randal shook his head. "I beg your pardon, Master, but I don't understand."

"Amaze me," the master wizard repeated. "Show me some magic. Let me see your best."

Randal looked at the dark man for a moment without speaking. *How am I supposed to amaze a master wizard?* he wondered. Finally he gave a sort of mental shrug and decided that he might as well do an easy color-spell. *Better something simple that I know will work,* he thought, *than something complicated that might fail.*

He held up his hands a few inches apart and

called up a ball of floating light—not the cold blue flame most wizards used for reading at night, but a warm yellow glow that shone against his upraised hands, making the long white scar across his right palm stand out in sharp relief.

Randal let the ball of light burn for a moment between his hands, and then set it free to circle around the room. He gave a mental command, and the globe split into first two and then four separate balls of light, each a different color. All four lights began to pulse with an inner rhythm, going bright and dim and bright again, faster and faster. At last they exploded, filling the air with silver sparkles that glittered and vanished before they hit the ground.

When the last sparkling flicker had died away, Randal let his hands fall to his sides and waited. The master wizard sat looking at him for a long time before he spoke.

"Two questions come to mind," the dark man said. "First—what is a northerner like yourself doing so far away from home? And second—why is a Schola-trained wizard with so much magical power at his disposal wasting his time on trivial games of sound and light?"

The questions cut closer to the bone than Randal liked. He drew a deep breath, and then let it out again slowly before he answered. "There are a master wizard and a powerful lord in Brecelande, both of whom want me dead. That's why I don't go back."

The dark man nodded. "A good reason," he said. "And truthfully spoken, as befits a wizard. But you haven't answered my second question."

16

Randal looked away and clenched his fists so hard that his right hand—the one with the scar—began to throb.

"I dealt with powerful magics once," he said. "A good friend died. Sounds and lights may be trivial, as you say . . . but they make people happy and they don't do any harm."

This time, the master wizard was silent for so long that Randal began to wonder if he had given offense with his abrupt reply. But when the dark man spoke, Randal heard no anger in his voice, only a certain amount of sympathy.

"Well, then, I am answered—though I suspect there's more to the story than you're telling." The master wizard smiled at Randal for the first time. "So—what should I call you while you're here?"

"My name is Randal," he said. "But why do you say 'while I'm here'?"

"His Grace the Prince gives me leave to dispose of illicit magicians however I choose," said the master wizard. "I do not bother him with the details. In your case, young Randal, I intend to make use of your abilities to ease my own burden."

"For how long?" Randal asked.

"A few weeks—until Midsummer, at least."

Randal relaxed a little. At least it didn't look like his visit to Peda was going to include a stay in the local jail, or worse. "What will I have to do?" he asked.

"You've already worked with magical entertainments," said the dark man. "They are, as I said, trivial—but it still takes a certain flair to do them well, and you seem to have the knack."

Once again, the master wizard regarded Randal over the tips of his steepled fingers. "Your presence here at this time is a stroke of good luck for me," he said, "since Prince Vespian is a passionate lover of theatrical entertainments. He finds them a relief from the cares of rulership, and for the most part I'm delighted to help make each performance something to remember. But at the moment, other matters are more pressing."

"I see," said Randal. "So I'm going to be one of the Prince's players whether I like it or not?"

"I'm afraid so, yes," said the dark man. Again, he smiled. "You won't go unrewarded, I promise you. The Prince is generous to those who serve him, and I myself will teach you everything I know about the uses of the magical Art for illusion and disguise. With that knowledge, you can take over for me in the theatre while I pursue my other duties."

Randal was silent for a moment. He wasn't quite certain how he should feel about the wizard's offer. *No, not an offer,* he corrected himself. *I'm not being given a choice. . . . But room and board here in the palace will make a pleasant change from life on the road—and learning new magic is what being a journeyman wizard is all about.*

"When do I begin?" he asked.

The master wizard clapped his hands sharply, and the door opened to admit the red-haired messenger whom Randal had followed earlier. The master wizard spoke to the man in Occitanian, and then turned back to Randal.

"This man will show you to your rooms in the east

wing," he told the journeyman. "We will begin our studies together tomorrow morning after breakfast. And one more thing—I notice you have some difficulties with the native speech. By morning, you will have found an answer to that particular problem."

Randal was silent for a moment, and then said, "Master . . . "

"Petrucio," said the dark man.

"Master Petrucio," Randal went on, "I would be glad to learn from you whatever you have to teach, and help you however I can—but what about my friend Lys? What happens to her?"

Petrucio smiled again. "The singer? She hasn't violated any laws that I know of and can come and go as she pleases. But if her singing is as good as I've heard it is, there will surely be a place for her in the Prince's troupe. Go now, and I will see you in the morning."

II.
Backstage Wizard

RANDAL SLEPT THAT night in more comfort than he had known since leaving his home for a life of wizardry. In fact, the chamber he was given in the servants' wing of the huge, rambling palace made his old room at Castle Doun look poor and cramped. Here, instead of a small, stone-walled room shared with his cousin Walter, he had a room of his own with wooden floors and white-plastered walls. Instead of a narrow, lumpy cot, he had a soft bed, and—as a final touch of luxury—the tall wardrobe closet standing in one corner was filled with new garments cut to his own measure.

He woke to sunlight coming through the glass windows onto his face and had no sooner finished dressing than a knock sounded at the door. He opened it and found another of the palace messengers waiting for him. The messenger bowed and said, "Master Petrucio bids you to break your fast with him, as soon as you are ready."

Randal's boyhood as first a page and then a squire in his uncle's castle had trained him well in courtly behavior. He bowed to the messenger in return and said, "Pray, lead on, sir."

A sudden thought brought the young wizard up short: *What language did we just use?* Then, recalling that Petrucio had promised him an answer to his problems with the local speech, Randal realized that the messenger had addressed him in Occitanian, and that he had answered in the same tongue.

Randal's guide left him outside the door to Petrucio's workroom. The journeyman opened the workroom door and found Petrucio waiting for him at a small table set for two.

"Good morning," said the master wizard as Randal entered. He waved a hand at the empty chair. "I trust you slept well?"

"Oh, yes," Randal said as he took his seat opposite Petrucio. "I could get too fond of living like this, I think—there's nothing like it in the northern lands."

Petrucio looked at him narrowly. "So you do plan to return some day, after all?"

"Back to Tarnsberg, at least," said Randal. "I'll have to, if I ever go before the Regents of the Schola to be examined for Mastery." *But that's a long way off,* he thought. *And I'm not sure I want to do the kind of magic that's required of a master wizard. It hurts too much.*

Before Randal could say more, the workroom door opened and a serving-man appeared, bearing a tray of silver topped with a silver lid. The man placed the tray on the table between the two wizards and removed the lid.

"Besides," Randal finished as the servant withdrew, "Brecelande is my home."

"Indeed," murmured the master wizard, as he looked over the dishes on the tray. "Excellent . . . nothing like buttered eggs for breakfast."

Randal nodded and turned his attention to the silverware at his own place. The knife and the spoon were familiar enough, even if more elegantly made than any he had seen, but the small, two-pronged utensil on the tablecloth beside them had him frowning in puzzlement.

He heard Petrucio chuckle. "It's called a fork. You still have a few things left to learn, I see."

"A fork," repeated Randal. He looked at the little tool for a moment longer, and then laid it back down beside the knife and spoon. "You spoke of having things to learn . . . but I have one thing less to learn than I thought I had. How is it that I speak the language of the people here, Master Petrucio, when yesterday I knew fewer than a dozen words of the tongue?"

"Come, now," said Petrucio with a smile. "Surely a journeyman wizard can recognize the effects of a spell."

"Yes," admitted Randal. "But why don't they use spells like that at the Schola? When I think of how many nights I stayed up late trying to learn how to say 'the candle is on the table' in the Old Tongue . . . "

Petrucio spooned some eggs onto his own plate, and then some onto Randal's. "The spell is a new one of my own, I'm afraid—I developed it out of my researches into the nature of language. Unfortunately, casting the spell requires a near-perfect under-standing of how a given language works, and such knowledge requires a lifetime of study."

Conversation lagged as the two wizards ate. When

breakfast was over, Petrucio leaned back and clapped his hands. The servant reappeared and cleared the table.

After the man had left, Petrucio looked over at Randal. "Some little while ago," said the master wizard, "I heard a strange story from the northlands, of an apprentice wizard who, in defiance of all tradition, killed a man with a sword. Have you heard of the case?"

Randal clenched his right hand over the raised scar that marred the palm and swallowed hard. *I can't lie to him. No true wizard can lie. If he does, then in the end his own magic will grow twisted and turn against him.* He met Petrucio's eyes, though it took an effort of will on his part. The master wizard's lean, dark face was unreadable.

"Yes," Randal said. "I was that apprentice."

Pride kept him from saying anything more, although he could have justified himself by saying that the blow had been struck out of desperation. He had been trapped by a master wizard who meant to offer his blood to the princes of the demonic realm, and he'd cut his own hand to the bone when he seized the blade.

I've already paid for breaking the law that says a wizard can't defend himself with steel, he thought. *If Prince Vespian's wizard still wants to throw me out on that account— well, I'm no worse off than I was at this time yesterday.*

But Petrucio was smiling. "Good," said the master wizard. "Then I can carry out a promise I made to the old friend who brought me that tale. He said that a journeyman wizard with a scarred hand might come here some day, and asked me to help him to the best of my ability."

Randal unclenched his fist. With the release of tension came curiosity—there weren't many people who were likely to be talking about him with a master wizard. "Your friend wouldn't have been named Madoc the Wayfarer, by any chance?"

Petrucio smiled. "By chance, yes."

"Master Madoc was the first wizard I ever met," said Randal, "and a good friend to me." For a moment he fell silent, remembering the traveling wizard who had filled the great hall of Castle Doun with marvelous creations of sound and light. Madoc had been a shrewd judge of character as well as a powerful wizard; if Master Petrucio called him friend, then the Occitanian wizard was someone worthy of trust and respect.

"I haven't seen Madoc since I left the Schola," said Randal finally. "How is he?"

"As footloose as ever," Petrucio said. "He didn't stay here long—but he talked of you fondly, and spoke well of your skills and ability."

"I hope I can live up to his good opinion of me," said Randal. "I'm afraid I wasn't always the most promising of apprentices."

"I think we can trust Master Madoc's judgment," Petrucio told him. "From what you showed me yesterday, I'd say you'll only need a little practice in the spells of color, disguise, and illusion, and then you'll be ready to spend the afternoon working with Prince Vespian's players."

The morning passed in the study of magical spells—in particular, the specialized illusions needed for the Prince's theater. About noon, a peculiar tapping on the inner door of Petrucio's workroom interrupted Randal's lessons—two knocks close together, a pause, and then three more.

Petrucio looked over at the door, and then back to where Randal stood. The young wizard had just completed the spell which magically altered his features to make him appear years older and pounds heavier. Petrucio frowned. "Randal," he said, "be a good lad and step into the library, will you? You can read anything you like—but don't come back in until I call you. See how long you can maintain your illusion."

Randal was baffled, but he followed Petrucio's orders. Still wearing another man's face and form, he went into the outer room, pulled out a book at random, and settled down into a chair beside the windows. He sat reading for quite some time, while voices—Petrucio's and another's—rose and fell behind the wizard's study door.

It was early afternoon before the door opened and Petrucio came out. "My apologies for interrupting your work like that," said the master wizard. "Sometimes such things happen. Now it's time you went to the theatre—when you get there, tell Vincente you're my new assistant and ask him to let you know what effects he's going to need for the Midsummer performance next month. Anything you can't manage on your own, we'll go over tomorrow morning."

Randal resumed his own appearance and went to do as he'd been told. Locating the theatre took him longer than he'd expected—for one thing, he'd never seen a theatre before. At last, he pushed open a pair of doors inlaid with ebony and mother-of-pearl—*black and silver must be the Prince's colors,* he thought, and paused for a moment on the threshold to look around in amazement.

The theatre was an immense, empty, high-ceilinged room, longer than it was wide, with a large stage at the far end. An arch of marble rose above the stage and supported heavy black curtains, now drawn back, that could be let down to conceal most of the stage area. Light came into the room from windows high up near the vaulted ceiling; wall brackets for candles showed how the room would be lit at night.

A group of men and women stood together down at the far end of the room. Among them Randal recognized Lys, busily talking with the same man who had escorted them to the palace. Today, instead of a velvet tunic, the man wore a plain white shirt and black hose, but there was no mistaking his bright red hair.

As Randal came down toward the stage, the red-headed man hurried forward to meet him, saying, "I see Master Petrucio's found us poor players a wizard of our own. I'm Vincente, by the way, and the rest of us you'll know soon enough. Tell me, can you do a ghost?"

Randal blinked. "A ghost?"

"We need one for the last act of the tragedy," Vincente explained. "Master Petrucio's been promising to work one up for us, but the Prince keeps him so busy at court that he doesn't have the time to spare."

"A ghost . . . " murmured Randal. He thought for a moment, and then cast the spell of visible illusion. A cloudy figure drifted down the length of the room from the double doors to the stage. "Something like that?"

"Not bad," said Vincente. "We'll have to give it the right face and walk, and work on getting a voice—but if that's what you can do on short notice, I think we're set."

"I told you Randy was good," Lys said to Vincente. She turned to Randal, her blue eyes alight. "You'll like working here, I know you will. Prince Vespian loves plays—that's why he built this theatre, and why he has his own troupe of actors, instead of hiring whoever comes through town."

Another of the actors nodded agreement. "Once the Prince had his own theatre inside the palace, every other ruler in Occitania had to do the same, or be out of fashion—but most places still hire traveling players to fill the stage. You won't see performances like ours anywhere else, I can tell you that. It's the rehearsals that do it, and you can't get those on the road."

"Speaking of rehearsals, Montalban," said Vincente, with a meaningful glance at the other actor, "it's time we all got back to work. Randal—for the first act, we need light that goes from dawn to early morning. Can you do that?"

"I think so," said the young wizard. "Where do you want me to be while I'm casting the spells?"

A few minutes later, Randal stood behind the black velvet curtain, calling up the rosy light of sunrise over the stage where Vincente and Montalban rehearsed the play's opening scene. By the time a distant gong sounded and the Prince's troupe broke off their work for the dinner hour, Randal had, by his own count, caused the sun to rise a dozen or more times. Vincente, it turned out, had definite ideas about just what color the sky should be at every line he and Montalban spoke—and Randal soon realized that while the actors only had to remember their own parts, the backstage wizard would have to know the entire play by heart.

Thank goodness the Schola taught me how to memorize things, he thought, as he went back to his room that evening. *I'll just have to pretend that a play is a peculiar sort of spell.*

The next few days passed in much the same manner as the first, with Randal studying magic in the morning hours and passing the afternoon with Vincente and the other actors in the Prince's theatre. Under Petrucio's guidance, Randal's skill at illusion increased until he could keep as many as four different actors disguised at once without feeling the strain.

Lys, for her part, seemed to be enjoying herself in her stage role as the hero's sister. For the first time in several years, the young singer was among people who spoke her own language and followed her own custom. More than that, she plainly reveled in the chance to be part of a troupe of actors. Sometimes, watching her at work during rehearsals, Randal wondered if she had found a permanent home among the Prince's players.

If she had, he knew that this time in Peda might be the last he would spend with Lys. For now, he was content to live in the palace and work with Master Petrucio—but he remained a journeyman wizard, bound by the rules of the Schola to wander the world in a quest for magical knowledge.

I won't be staying here, he admitted to himself a few days after his arrival, as he stood in the theatre with Vincente, watching Lys and Montalban rehearsing a scene together. *Not if I'm going to be a master wizard. If I want to make myself ready to return to Tarnsberg and the Schola, I won't be able to keep away from the open road forever. Lys, though . . . this is the life she was born to.*

"Watch this bit," said Vincente quietly at Randal's elbow, interrupting his thoughts. "The entrance. You've only seen it with Montalban being lowered down on a rope from the prop-loft. Today we're trying the trap door from the under-stage—see if you think it's any better."

Randal nodded and turned his attention to Montalban, who was making his entrance as the wicked uncle. "Neither way is going to look like a magic portal," he said finally. "I'm surprised that the Prince didn't have Master Petrucio construct a portal or two to go with all those trap doors."

"He thought of it," said Vincente. "But the theatre wasn't newly built from the ground up. It was made over from an older wing of the palace."

"I see," said Randal. Magic portals, if built by a wizard who wanted something permanent, had to be constructed along with the building they were part of—and a temporary portal called for more power than even a master wizard could afford to spend for anything short of life and death.

Randal considered the stage for a moment. "The trap-door entrance is the better of the two," he decided. "But it still doesn't look much like real magic."

"It doesn't need to," said Vincente. "Give us a flash of light and a loud bang, and that'll cover up anything awkward."

Randal nodded and went back to watching the actors. When the scene was finished, Lys came forward to the edge of the stage.

"How did it look?" she asked.

"Better than the last time," said Vincente. "I was afraid we'd have to cut the scene, but we'll get it right yet."

The black-haired singer sat down on the lip of the stage with her feet dangling over the edge. "Good," she said. She stretched, catlike, and then smiled at Vincente. "You can't imagine," she said, "how good it feels to be acting again. I've been singing, mostly, for about three years now, with a bit of acrobatics thrown in for good measure—but I was born into a family of actors, and acting is what I do best."

Vincente smiled back at her. "You make a fine addition to the troupe. . . . Will you be staying with us here in Peda after the Midsummer performance?"

Randal held his breath and looked away, not wanting to hear his suspicions confirmed. But Lys shook her head regretfully and said, "I don't know. It's good to be back with my own people, and the Prince isn't a bad man to serve. But Randy and I have been partners almost since we met. He saved my life, you know—I stay as long as he does, no more."

Randal felt a warm glow of surprise. He'd always been grateful for Lys's friendship but hadn't realized that she herself put such a high value on it.

"And besides," Lys continued, "there's something about Brecelande. The song hasn't come to its final verse, if you follow me." She hesitated, as if searching for the right words. "My family wanted to go to that country, and I feel, somehow, that I have to finish what they began."

Randal was puzzled, both by what Lys said and by the hesitant way in which she spoke, so unlike her usual self-assured tone. Before he could say anything, however, the doors at the far end of the theatre opened. A messenger in the Prince's black-and-silver livery hurried down to the group standing in front of the stage. The man sketched a hasty bow to Randal and Lys, and then beckoned Vincente aside.

The actor stood for a little while, listening as the messenger spoke in a rapid undertone. After the man had finished, Vincente turned back to the others.

"Your pardon," he said, "but it seems I'm urgently needed elsewhere. We'll take up again tomorrow where we left off." The red-haired actor bowed and walked quickly away.

Randal watched him go. A puzzled frown began to form between the young wizard's brows. For some reason, Vincente's abrupt departure had called to his mind the unexpected knock at the door of Petrucio's workroom his first day in the palace. That time, the master wizard had sent him out of the room with no more explanation than Vincente had just given.

Maybe it's just because I'm a foreigner here, he thought. *But I get the feeling sometimes that there's more going on in Peda than meets the eye.*

III.

Hidden Ways

BETWEEN STUDY AND practice, the next few weeks went by swiftly. As Midsummer Night grew closer, the rehearsals became more intense. Vincente, while unfailingly cheerful and courteous, was just as unfailingly reluctant to settle for less than everyone's best effort, and often Randal didn't return to his chamber in the east wing until well after dark.

The last rehearsal before Midsummer proved especially long and exhausting. Randal made the illusory sun come up over the opening scene again and again, and walked the transparent, moaning ghost up and down the length of the theatre more times than he could count, before Vincente called for a break.

A cool stone jar of mint-and-honey-flavored water stood on a trestle table backstage; Randal dipped himself out a mugful and drained it in one long, grateful swallow. *Disguises and illusions may be trivial,* he thought as he filled his mug again, *but do enough of them at a stretch and they leave you just as drained as throwing a lightning bolt or looking into the future.*

Still carrying his mug, he joined Lys and Vincente out near the front of the stage. The two actors and the journeyman wizard watched as a half-dozen palace servants went in and out through a small door beneath the stage, carrying out cushioned benches from the storeroom where they were kept and setting them up in rows.

Randal tried to guess from the seats how many people were going to be watching the Midsummer performance. The number startled him. "Where are all these people going to be coming from?" he asked Vincente.

"Everywhere," answered the red-haired actor, with a broad gesture. "These *are* the Midsummer Revels, after all, and our Prince has a reputation to uphold. All the notable families of Peda are invited, the other Occitanian states are sending ambassadors—you'll even see people from as far away as Brecelande."

Randal took a sip from his mug. "I didn't know the merchants of Peda traveled that far north."

Peda's merchants don't trade much farther away than Widsegard," admitted Vincente. "But His Grace, our Sovereign Ruler, has been known to lend some of Peda's gold—at a moderate rate of interest, naturally—to one or another of your northern earls."

Lys looked curious. "Whatever for?"

"Wars cost money," Randal said. "Supplies . . . weapons . . . pay for the mercenaries . . . " He thought of the chest of gold coins that his uncle kept in the strongroom at Castle Doun, in case one day the unrest in Brecelande brought more trouble than Doun's knights and men-at-arms could deal with

34

alone. "In Brecelande, there's always fighting going on someplace—and when there's fighting, the winner takes all. If the Prince supports the right side, he gets his money back with interest."

"So he does," admitted Vincente. "I can't say I care much for that part of it myself. But I've heard that our Prince—may Fortune continue to smile on him—has a tender conscience, and that only those with just causes may borrow from Peda's treasury. An envoy from Brecelande is here right now, in fact, on just such a mission."

"Do you know his name?" Randal asked curiously, not really expecting an answer. *And even if I get one,* he thought, *who's to say I'll recognize him? It's been a long time since I left home.*

Vincente shrugged. "Ambassadors and actors don't mix, I'm afraid. But he's said to be an honorable man."

Lys was looking doubtful. "Honorable or not," she told Vincente, "I still think that Peda gets the better part of the bargain."

Randal was forced to agree. He could see that Prince Vespian was rich—everything about the palace spelled wealth, from the ample meals in the servants' hall to the marble statues in the formal gardens. He had also seen the same prosperity reigning in the city outside the palace walls. Even the poorest townspeople here looked happier and better-fed than the well-off in northern cities like Tattinham and Cingestoun.

He stood for a while in silence, watching the palace servants set up more benches. A commotion at one of the side doors drew his attention, and he turned to see four of the strongest men bringing in something large and heavy—a massive high-backed throne with leaping dolphins for the armrests and a snarling lion's head on the back, all carved from a single block of some dark wood.

Randal nodded toward the servants wrestling with the huge chair. "I suppose that belongs to the Prince."

Vincente nodded. "Ugly, isn't it? And uncomfortable, or so I'm told. But you have to admit it looks impressive."

Before Randal could answer, a shout came from the servants bringing in the throne—one of them had stumbled against the corner of a bench. As Randal watched, the man went down on one knee and lost his grip on the back edge of the throne. The other three men fought to keep their burden from going over, but in vain—the heavy chair swayed, toppled, and came down with a crash on the fallen man, trapping his leg under the weight of solid wood.

The man screamed. Vincente leaped down from the stage and reached the overturned chair in three long strides.

"Lys!" the actor shouted over his shoulder as he ran. "Fetch the palace healer, and hurry! Randal, come help us shift this thing!"

But even from his place on the stage, the young wizard could see bright red blood spurting from the man's leg where the weight of the throne pressed down. *The bone's broken,* Randal thought, *and it's cut the artery. He'll bleed to death before a healer gets here.*

36

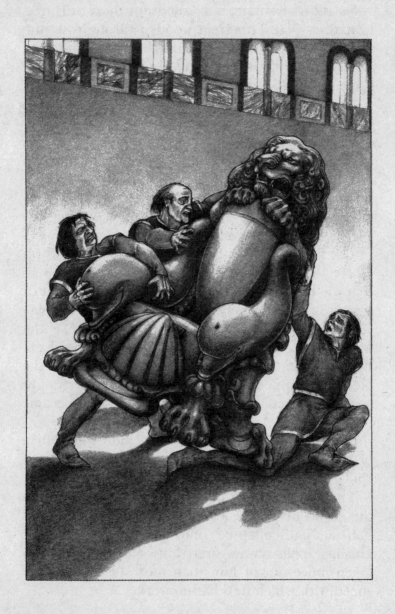

He didn't hesitate, but called out the words of a levitation-spell. The great wooden throne rose into the air. By the time it hit the floor again several yards away, Randal had already jumped from the stage to join the group around the injured man.

"I know the healing-spells," he said. "I can help him."

The others drew back, and Randal passed his hands along the man's leg, feeling for damage with the wizardly senses that went beyond sight and touch. *Mend the cut artery first, to stop the bleeding . . . then bring the pieces of bone into place and start them growing back together again . . . then build his strength and ease the pain.*

The healing-spells that Randal had learned from Master Balpesh were still fresh in his mind—spells that the master wizard had called the high point of the wizard's art, even though few of the Schola's wizards chose to follow them. Randal spoke the words and felt the man sink into the healing sleep. As Vincente, Lys, and the others watched, the bleeding stopped and the broken leg grew straight again. The man's breathing deepened and became more regular.

Randal stood. "He'll sleep until he's well. Put a blanket over him—sometimes healing produces a chill."

The young wizard moved a few steps away from the crowd of people around the sleeping man and half-sat, half-collapsed onto one of the benches. Healing-spells always tired him, and this one had taken more out of him than most, because of the speed with which he'd had to work.

After a minute or two, Vincente came over and sat down on the bench beside him. The red-haired actor's face was almost as pale as the injured man's had been, and his expression was sober.

"That was a good thing you did," he told Randal. "We're glad you were with us today—but if you can do magic like that, then why in the name of Fortune aren't you working as somebody's court wizard instead of providing stage effects for a troupe of actors?"

"I'm only a journeyman, remember," said Randal, with a grimace. "Hardly court-wizard material."

"The rank doesn't matter," Vincente persisted. "There're more princely courts in Occitania looking for wizardly aid than there are master wizards to supply it. You could be a power in the state, wherever you decided to go—our own Master Petrucio is Vespian's right arm, here in Peda."

Randal shook his head violently and clasped his hands together. The scar across his right palm throbbed from the pressure. "I don't want to be 'a power in the state,' thank you," he said. "I've seen what comes of meddling with the great magics and trying to cure the world's problems . . . and I don't want to do it anymore."

Lys had joined the two of them during this speech. Now she laid a hand on Randal's shoulder. "Let him be, Vincente," she said before the actor could speak. "He's got his reasons. I was there, and I know."

The actor rose to his feet. "Not a word more, then. Let's finish shoving His Grace's blasted chair into place and get on with our rehearsal. . . . Are you coming, Randal?"

It was almost midnight when Vincente finally declared himself more or less satisfied with the troupe's performance. Randal was yawning outright as he said good night to Lys and the others and started back to his room.

The halls were dark and quiet around him as he made his way through the palace. Elsewhere in the great building, the nobility might stay awake and revel into the small hours, but in the servants' quarters only the Prince's actors—and their journeyman wizard—were still moving about. With that thought uppermost in his mind, he rounded the last corner and almost bumped into a palace messenger going the other way.

"Are you looking for someone?" Randal asked the man, feeling suddenly anxious. A messenger sent at this hour couldn't mean anything good. "Does Master Petrucio need me?"

The messenger shook his head and hurried on without speaking. Randal watched him go. The young wizard's sense of puzzlement grew as the messenger's black-and-silver livery blended into the shadows and vanished. *Odd,* thought Randal. *Usually those fellows are models of courtesy, but this one didn't even apologize for almost running into me.*

Randal shrugged. *And who do I think I am, to want the Prince's servants bowing every time I walk by? I'm only a penniless journeyman, not even a permanent member of the Prince's household—I'd better start remembering that more often.*

Still, he couldn't help feeling uneasy. And when he undid the locking-spell he'd placed on the door of his room, he became even more concerned: The spell gave way far too easily, as if it had been broken and then recast by another. For a moment, he paused with his hand still on the doorknob, fighting the impulse to turn and run.

This is how the trouble in Widsegard began, he thought, *with the lock on my room broken and someone waiting inside.*

Then he drew a deep breath, straightened his shoulders, and opened the door.

The room was just as he had left it. The cold blue glow of his witchlight showed no one lying in wait. Feeling a bit foolish, he pulled open the door of the tall wardrobe closet and found nobody lurking there, either. But his investigations did tell him something else—while nothing was out of place, the whole room had been thoroughly searched.

Something strange is going on, thought Randal, as he prepared to recast the locking-spell. He made the charm a stronger one this time, so that he would sense any attempt to break it, even in his sleep. Then, feeling as secure as he could under the circumstances, he climbed into bed. His last thought as slumber overtook him was that he would have to consult Master Petrucio in the morning.

At breakfast the next day, over crusty rolls and butter, Randal said, "I think someone searched my room last night."

Petrucio looked interested. "Indeed? Did you have the usual door-guards up on your room?"

"Yes," said Randal, "and door-guards were still there when I came back from rehearsals. But I could tell that someone had broken the spell and cast it again." He paused to go through his memories of the night before. "And another thing—on my way back to the east wing, I ran into a man going the other way. He wore the palace livery, but I think he may have been a stranger just the same."

The master wizard frowned. "Can you show him to me—create his image as you would on the stage?"

"I'll try," said Randal. He turned back again to his memories of the stranger. When the man stood before him in his mind's eye, Randal spoke the words of visual illusion, and a clear image of the messenger appeared before them in the middle of the workroom.

Petrucio rose from the breakfast table and walked all around the figure. "You're sure?" he asked.

"As sure as I can be."

The master wizard nodded. "I was afraid that something like this might happen," he said to Randal. "Close down the illusion and come with me."

He turned and pushed against one of the panels on the inner wall of his workroom. The polished wood slid to the right with a faint click, revealing a dark opening. *A secret passage,* thought Randal, with a thrill of excitement. *I wonder where it leads.*

Petrucio had already stepped through the doorway and was looking back at Randal. The young wizard smiled to himself at his own eagerness—*wherever the passage goes, it looks like I'm about to find out*—and went in after him.

The master wizard slid the door closed. Then he called up a cold-flame for light and began to stride

42

along the passage, with Randal hurrying after him. At last, they came to a low door. Petrucio pulled it open, and Randal realized that they were looking into the next room through the back of a fireplace. Before he could say anything, Petrucio ducked under the mantelpiece and stepped out onto the carpet.

Randal followed and looked around the room curiously. On one wall, a black-and-silver heraldic device of lions and dolphins hung above a set of double doors. At the other end of the room, another set of doors opened onto one of the palace's many corridors.

Again Petrucio gestured at Randal to follow. The master wizard strode over to the doors beneath the dolphins and lions and pushed them apart without knocking. They swung open to reveal a spacious room with high windows, containing only a few chairs and a writing desk. A dark man wearing plain, almost severe clothing lounged in a comfortable chair before one of the windows, reading from a small scroll.

The man looked up as Petrucio walked in. The master wizard bowed and held the pose. Randal hesitated a moment, caught by surprise. Then his old training as a squire in his uncle's castle took over. He, too, bowed and waited to see what would happen.

The man spoke in a quiet, pleasant-sounding voice. "Well, old friend, what brings you here today?"

"It's just as I feared, Your Grace," Petrucio said, straightening as he spoke. "The Duke is up to his old tricks."

43

Randal straightened as well when he caught the wizard's movement, lifting his head in time to see the man put aside the scroll and look keenly at them. From Petrucio's words and actions, Randal realized that they had come into the presence of Prince Vespian the Magnificent, Sovereign Ruler of Peda.

So that's what he looks like, thought Randal, with an odd feeling of disappointment. *Not particularly magnificent, really . . . There's nothing handsome about him, and even Vincente's a better dresser.*

Then Randal stole a second glance and reconsidered. In spite of his plain appearance, the Prince had an air of authority about him that reminded Randal of his friend Madoc the Wayfarer. Master Madoc looked and dressed like an uncivilized tribesman from the far north, but no one who met him ever doubted that he was one of the most powerful wizards in Brecelande. In the same way, Randal realized, anyone who looked twice at Vespian would know him for what he was—the absolute ruler of Peda and all the surrounding territories.

The Prince looked from Petrucio to Randal, and then back to the master wizard. "You will, of course, find out what the Duke is planning and thwart him."

"Of course," said Petrucio, with another, briefer bow.

"Then good day, wizard. We appreciate your efforts."

Randal and Petrucio turned to go but stopped at the sound of the Prince's voice saying, "One more thing, Master Petrucio."

Petrucio turned again. "Your Grace?"

"Just once, I wish you would knock." The man chuckled, as if to show that he was joking.

Petrucio chuckled, too. "If I knocked, Your Grace, how would you know it was I?"

Still smiling, the master wizard departed with Randal close on his heels. They entered the secret passage behind the fireplace and walked back through the narrow ways to Petrucio's workroom.

To Randal's surprise, the room was occupied—but the lean, plainly dressed man who sat writing at Petrucio's desk was certainly no wizard. The stranger wore a serviceable dagger at his belt, and the long, narrow-bladed sword at his side had a grip worn smooth with use. *I don't know who he is,* thought Randal, *but he looks dangerous.*

At their entrance, the man looked up from his writing. The master wizard, seemingly unsurprised by the presence of a stranger in his workroom, raised a dark eyebrow at his visitor and said only, "Back so soon?"

The man nodded. "New developments." He looked at Randal, then back at Petrucio, and handed a scrap of parchment to the master wizard. "It's all in here."

Petrucio scanned the parchment. "It isn't much."

"I can get more information," said the stranger, "but you know where I'd have to go to do it."

"Handle the affair as you think best," said the master wizard. "But be discreet about it."

"Right," said the man. "I'll be off, then." He stood and left the room.

After he had left, silence filled the workroom. Petrucio looked at the closed door for a few seconds, then turned to Randal. "Today you've been shown things that most folk in Peda never suspect," said the master wizard. "Now I need your assistance. Will you give it?"

Randal thought for a moment. "If I can," he said finally. "In every honorable way."

Petrucio smiled—Randal thought for a second that he looked relieved. "Very good," said the wizard. "By now, you've probably guessed that I do more than keep His Grace amused."

"I'd wondered what you were doing while I was working on magical disguises for Vincente and the rest," admitted Randal. "But what does that have to do with my room being searched? I just came to Peda this summer, and I haven't got the faintest idea what's going on around here."

"What you know or don't know remains a mystery to most people," said Petrucio. "And you are, after all, a wizard. They were probably just trying to find out as much as they could about you from your possessions."

Randal gave a brief laugh. "They wouldn't have found out much—except for my spell-book, I don't have anything here that didn't come from the palace to start with. And the spell-book stays in my pocket."

"Wise of you," said Petrucio, "since—as you may also have guessed—there are those in Peda who don't share most people's love for His Grace. Because Vespian employs me to inform him of their plots, and because you are known to be my assistant, you will have come under their suspicion as well."

Randal considered the odd happenings and conversations of the past few hours. "You think that somebody is conspiring to overthrow the Prince?"

"I know they are," said Petrucio. The master wizard sighed. "It's a problem of long standing, I'm afraid. The Prince is a kindhearted man— sentimental, one might call him. He coddles his greatest enemy, gives him a villa outside the city walls, provides him with money and all that he might require. And how does this fellow repay that kindness? With constant plotting and treachery. But Prince Vespian is sentimental, as I said. He refuses to have Bartolomeo put to death."

"Bartolomeo?" asked Randal. "Who's he?"

"Vespian's brother," said Petrucio. "His identical twin brother. Some fifteen minutes younger and as wicked at the Prince is good."

IV.
Secret Mission

SO THE PRINCE has a twin brother he doesn't trust, thought Randal. *That would make things difficult for His Grace.*

"I must admit I'd rest easier at night knowing that Duke Bartolomeo had met with a fatal accident," the master wizard went on, "but Prince Vespian has expressly forbidden anyone in Peda to harm his brother. As a result, I'm often kept busier by the Duke's plottings than I'd really like."

Randal looked at Petrucio. "I said I'd help if I could," he said, "and I will."

"Good," said Petrucio. "Do you suppose you could cast one of those theatrical spells upon yourself, so that you look nothing like the young man who spends his afternoons with the Prince's actors?"

Randal thought for a moment. Since his first day of study with Master Petrucio, he'd never tried maintaining a magical disguise on his own person for very long, since—except for mirrors—he didn't have any means of checking on his appearance once the illusion was in place. But the principle was the same, whether he cast the spell on himself or on another, and he'd been getting a lot of practice over the past few weeks.

"Yes," he said finally. "I can do it."

"Then listen carefully," said Petrucio. He read from the scrap of parchment the other man had given him. "'A tall man, but thin and stringy; blue-eyed; short black hair mixed with gray; a small, pointed beard; dresses after the local fashion but carries no weapons.'"

"That's not much to go on," said Randal.

"Just do the best you can," Petrucio told him.

Randal closed his eyes and began to work the spell—taking Petrucio's brief description and letting his imagination play with it until an entire man emerged from the few short phrases. Then he thought, rather than spoke aloud, the words that set the illusion in place around him.

He didn't feel any different, but when he stole a glance at his reflection in the polished brass base of a candlestick, a stranger looked back. *It worked,* he thought with relief. Aloud, he said, "Will this do?"

"Close enough," said the master wizard. "Now— can you keep that illusion going all day, if you must?"

"After all the work with Vincente and the rest of them for tonight's performance," Randal said, "I'd better be able to."

"Good," said Petrucio. "I knew I could count on you." The master wizard picked up a piece of white chalk from the table and handed it to Randal. "Now—go to the fountain in Peda's market square."

"I remember the place," said Randal. "Lys and I

performed there our first two days in the city."

"Then you know that the fountain has a flight of steps leading up to the basin," the master wizard replied. "Use that chalk to mark an X on the left end of the third step on the north side. Then go to the nearest inn, take a seat, and have lunch. Here are five silver pennies. Use all of them to pay for your meal."

"*All* of them?" Randal pocketed the pennies—new-minted silver, marked with Prince Vespian's seal and image—but he still felt curious. A single copper coin would buy a meal and lodging in most of the inns in Brecelande, and even here in the southlands the prices weren't so high that a man had to pay for his meals in silver.

"All," said Petrucio firmly.

"And then what?"

"See what happens," said the master wizard, "and return when you feel you should. Before the performance at midnight, certainly."

When I feel I should. Randal sighed inwardly. "How will I know when that is?"

"Come, come," said Petrucio, with a flash of annoyance. "A Schola-trained journeyman should know better than to ask a question like that—there are too many possible answers. But unless I've misjudged, you'll know the time when it arrives."

Petrucio went over to the workroom's inner door and pushed it open. Randal saw that it opened not onto a palace corridor, but to the outside, with the rest of the city of Peda sloping away downhill.

"Off you go," said Petrucio. "I'll be waiting in my study when you return."

Randal stepped across the threshold and heard the door close behind him. He turned back and faced the blank outer wall of Prince Vespian's palace. No door was visible. Randal looked about, trying to memorize the location for his return, then started out for the city and the market square below.

As always, when he left the palace grounds and went out into the streets of Peda, Randal marveled at the buildings he saw around him—large, open, and airy, with thin walls of soft stone or brick. No one in the north would have dared to put up such beautiful but flimsy buildings. He remembered his uncle's castle of Doun, in the middle of Brecelande. The walls there were granite, cut in huge blocks many feet thick, to make the castle strong in case of attack.

Remembering Castle Doun made Randal feel homesick. It had been several months since he'd left Brecelande, longer than that since he'd last been in Tarnsberg, where the Schola was—and he hadn't been inside the walls of Castle Doun since he was not quite thirteen. He hadn't heard a voice speaking in the accents of his homeland since his friend Nicolas Wariner had died and he had turned south from Widsegard.

With Master Petrucio's language-spell on me, Randal thought, *I don't even sound right to myself.*

By the time he reached the bottom of the hill, he found himself willing to trade Peda and all its riches for the taste of a brimming mug of dark brown northlands cider or the sound of his cousin Walter's voice. The melancholy mood clung to him as he made his way through the streets. But Peda's market square—a large open space thronged with people buying and selling everything from fruits and vegetables to bowls of beaten gold—was an excellent antidote to gloom. In spite of himself, Randal felt his spirits lighten as he pushed through the crowd to the base of the fountain and climbed the steps.

On the third step he sat, stretching his legs out with the air of a fellow who had all day to spend watching the citizens of Peda do their marketing. He reached into his pocket and closed his fingers around the chalk Petrucio had given him. After a little more time had passed, he bent over as if to adjust his shoe and traced a cross on the marble step.

So far, so good, he thought. *Now for the next part.*

Finding the closest inn wasn't easy—the north face of the square alone had three. Still, it wasn't impossible. One of them, The Egret, was clearly—*almost* clearly—the closest of the lot.

Randal stood up again, crossed the square to The Egret, and walked in. He stood for a minute just inside the door, blinking as his eyes adjusted to the dim light. The inn's common-room was half full of patrons and appeared clean and prosperous. Randal walked up to a large man in a white apron who was busy wiping bread crumbs off a recently vacated table.

"I'll have lunch," Randal said. He pulled the five silver pieces out of his pocket and slapped them down onto the table.

The man scooped up the coins without missing a

beat. "You'll be wanting the special, then," he said. "Come with me."

Randal followed the innkeeper into a smaller room, where more tables stood ready. So far, Randal seemed to be the only customer in this part of the inn. Then the innkeeper departed, closing the door to the common-room behind him and leaving Randal alone.

The young wizard sat and waited for what seemed a long time. When nothing happened, he began to wonder, nervously, if he'd picked the right place after all. The Dolphin had been his second choice—what if Petrucio had meant him to go there instead? While he was still caught in his indecision, the door from the common-room opened again. A serving-maid bustled in with a plate of meat and cheese and a tumbler of cool water.

Randal ate hungrily—breakfast had been cut short. The meal wasn't as fine as what he had been getting in the palace, but it was equally filling. Life here in Peda, he reflected, was a sharp contrast to most of his experiences since he had walked away from Castle Doun to study magic.

Madoc the Wayfarer had been right about the life of a traveling wizard. "You'll be hungry more often than you're fed," he'd said to Randal, "and spend more time in danger on the road than safe under a roof." The past few weeks, on the other hand, had been the most comfortable Randal had ever known. It had taken the searching of his room to make him wonder if something was going seriously wrong in Peda—something that he didn't understand.

The possibility frightened him. *Because Madoc was right about everything else, too,* Randal thought. *"Maybe you'll survive it all," he told me, "but most of your friends will have died a long time before." And now Nick's dead, for no better reason than that I asked for help and he gave it.*

"Lys," Randal muttered under his breath. "What about Lys?" Risking himself was one matter—but if another friend was to suffer for his choices, that would be more than he could bear. Randal looked at the heavy glass tumbler of water sitting on the table. The means were at hand to take a look into the future—why not try it? He picked up the tumbler, cleared his mind, and spoke the words of the scrying-spell.

For a long time, the water in the glass remained clear and untroubled. Then, down in the bottom, a bloom of color appeared, the red of a flowering rose, or a sunset, or blood. *Blood,* thought Randal, as the color spread and filled his vision, until the world seemed full of it. Then he drew back from the color and saw that the blood was a river flowing through a parched and dusty land.

He rose still higher above the river, like an eagle searching for its prey, and saw that the river was really a rope, blood red, tying two men together. They both wore masks, plain white masks with crude features drawn on them, and both were dressed in rich robes—one in a white cloak with a black lining, and the other in a black cloak with a white lining.

Back and forth they pulled on the red rope. The brown color that Randal had seen as the banks of a river now changed and became the boards of the stage in the Prince's palace. Then Randal saw that the rope was tied around the neck of the wizard Petrucio, and the two men pulling on it were strangling him.

As Randal watched, he seemed to hear Madoc the Wayfarer speaking in his mind: "You're the one who can stop them, lad. Magic was meant to be used, not wasted."

"I can't," murmured Randal, unable to look away from the struggle below. "The price is too high—I know that now."

"High or low," said the well-remembered voice, "we all have to pay it. That's what makes us wizards."

The sound of a latch opening jolted Randal back to reality. He was in the tavern, looking into a glass of plain water, and the door was opening. All that Randal could see in the water was his reflection, and the face was his own. Hastily he recast the spell of illusion, hoping that the disguise would take effect in time.

The door opened, and a man stepped in.

"Yes?" Randal said, in tones as bored as he could manage. He turned his head to look at the man who had entered. *Well-dressed, and he carries a sword, but he's not in the palace livery . . . now, what made me think of that?* Then he remembered. *That's the man I saw last night, when my room was searched.*

"We only now got the news that you had arrived," the man said. "You found the terms satisfactory, I hope?"

Who does he think I am, anyway, Randal thought,

and what are those terms he's talking about? Then another thought came to him. *How on earth am I to continue this disguise business without telling any lies? No true wizard can tell a lie and ever trust his own magic again.*

Instead, he told the truth—carefully, and in small pieces. "I've been waiting here a long time," he said. "And I want to get on with my business."

"Excellent," the man said. "Come with me."

The man escorted the young wizard through the common-room and out into the market square. Randal saw that the day was older than he'd expected—the time he'd spent gazing into the clear water had seemed brief, but now the sky between the buildings was dark, while lower down, Peda's torches and lanterns filled the streets with flickering light.

Do they miss me at the palace? Randal thought. *The actors will be getting ready soon for tonight's performance and they expect me to help them set up.*

"The coach is ready," the man said. "Is there anything you need to take care of before we go?"

"No," Randal replied truthfully, and the man led the way into a nearby alley. A second man stood waiting in the darkness, holding the heads of a team of horses hitched to a tall coach.

"It took you long enough," he said as they appeared. "I get nervous every time I come here."

Randal and the man from the inn climbed into the coach. The driver closed the door after them, and Randal heard him climbing up onto his box. Then, with a cry of "Gee-ah!" the coach lurched forward.

They drove out of the city and into the farmland that surrounded Peda. *Where are they taking me?* Randal wondered. *I saw the Prince's theatre in my vision, but we're headed in the opposite direction.*

After a while, they passed through the gates of a farm and drove into one of the outbuildings. Inside the building, another coach awaited them. This one, Randal saw, had heavy black curtains drawn over the windows, so that no one outside could tell who the coach carried, and no one inside would be able to tell where it was going. Randal and his guide got into the second coach and once more drove into the night.

With the curtains drawn, riding in the coach was like sitting inside the toe of a boot. Fortunately, Randal reflected, it took more than a few layers of cloth to confuse a wizard about which way was which. He'd drawn enough magic circles by now—each one exactly labeled at the four directions—that he could find true north by his magical senses alone, even on a dark night.

The coach was traveling in a large circle, heading back in the direction of Peda. Randal kept his knowledge to himself and waited. Eventually the sound of the carriage changed, and the vehicle swayed, slowed, and stopped.

The door of the carriage swung open, and Randal and his guide stepped down into a graveled courtyard. Surrounding the courtyard was what by daylight would be a garden in the formal style favored here in the south, and beyond the bushes and statues rose the moonlit walls of a country villa.

Armed men lounged about the dark courtyard. Randal saw that they carried heavy killing swords—more like the ones he had trained with during his days as a squire in Brecelande than the lighter weapons of Vespian's court.

Randal and his guide walked through the gardens and into the long front hall of the villa. The walls here, like the ones in the palace, were plastered and painted. Alcoves here and there held bronze and marble statues in heroic poses. The guide led the way to a door where two more men-at-arms stood guard.

Randal and his companion went past the guards into a small room furnished with a table and chairs. Light from lanterns in the four corners shone down on the center of the room, where a man stood in chains. With a sense of shock, Randal recognized the prisoner as the man he'd seen in Petrucio's hidden workroom only that morning.

Suddenly, the young wizard felt frightened. So far, all this had been an adventure—mysterious, perhaps, but exciting. Now a cold wind blew through him, and the pleasure went out of what he was doing.

"We know your reputation well, Master Edmond," said Randal's guide. "But my master needs proof." He pointed to the chained figure. "A spy we caught this afternoon. Kill him."

For a moment, Randal couldn't answer—he was too busy keeping his face from showing the dismay he felt as one thing after another fell into place in his mind. *He called me "Master," and he can see that I don't carry steel. These people must have brought a wizard into Peda to do their killing for them . . . and they think I'm he.*

Randal looked more closely at the chained man and saw that he had been savagely beaten. Still, the prisoner drew himself up as best he could within his chains and met Randal's gaze without flinching.

I can't kill him, thought Randal. *But if I refuse, these other fellows will kill him anyway, and probably do their best to kill me. Maybe I could make it past all those swordsmen out in the courtyard—but not without killing some of them, too.*

No, he realized, there was only one way out of this one. He called all his magic to him and cast the spell of visual illusion—and a couple of other spells as well.

"Fiat!" he shouted as a lightning bolt streaked from his fingers to the manacled man, struck him, and splashed blue-white fire throughout the room.

Thunder boomed. The man staggered and fell, his body crumbling into ash. A high wind blew through the closed chamber, picking up the little pile of ashes. They swirled for a moment in the air and vanished. All that remained were the empty chains.

The man who had guided Randal was silent for a moment. Then he spoke. "I thank you, Master Edmond. I'm sure my master will be well satisfied with your efforts."

As long as nobody walks behind the chairs, Randal thought. *A healing-spell tends to make a man sleep deeply, and an invisibility-spell will last only as long as he doesn't move. But if they find him, then we've both had it.*

But the guide was already moving, leading Randal to a inner door. They passed into another room, where a man stood waiting. Randal nearly gasped. He had seen this man before, only this morning. He was once more in the presence of Prince Vespian.

Then he looked more carefully. No, there were differences. Small ones—more in the man's expression and the way he held himself than in anything physical—but real differences nonetheless. *It's not the Prince. So it must be—*

Randal bowed low.

"I am here, Duke Bartolomeo," he said.

V.

Into the Dungeons

RANDAL ROSE FROM his bow to encounter Bartolomeo's unblinking gaze.

"No, Master Edmond," Vespian's brother said. "Not 'Duke.' Practice calling me 'Prince'—since, with your help, I soon will be."

Randal bowed again to cover his shock. *So that's what the vision meant . . . twin brothers struggling . . . and I've fallen right into their feud.* "As you will, my lord Prince."

Bartolomeo smiled and turned to the messenger. "This fellow will do, Carvelli. Show him to his room, and return. We have much to discuss."

"Come, Master Edmond," Carvelli said. "Your chamber is already prepared."

The Duke's messenger led Randal back out through the other room. The young wizard glanced over at the spot where the manacled man had stood. With an inward sigh of relief, he saw that his former victim was still invisible—and presumably still unconscious. The simple invisibility-spell would break as soon as the subject moved.

I've got to get back here before he wakes up, thought Randal. *He's one of Prince Vespian's men. If he's recaptured, it will be the worse for him. And for me.*

The young wizard followed Carvelli through the passageways to a sumptuously decorated room furnished with a curtained bed and a carved marble washstand—but no windows. There the messenger left him. The door closed behind Carvelli, and the bolt snicked into place.

I have to get back to the palace and warn Master Petrucio, Randal thought as he began to prowl around the room. No other doors presented themselves, and the fireplace was blocked a few feet above the grate by close-set iron bars. This was a luxurious prison, but a prison nonetheless.

He tried the door. *Locked. Why am I not surprised?* He laid an ear to the crack. *Someone's standing there, trying to be quiet. A guard—I think.*

Randal cast the spell of magical resonance. The spell would come back like an echo from any magical object or spell nearby, and from any other wizard.

A faint trace of magical energy returned to him on the spell's echo, but the power was weak, coming from nothing more than a healwife or a self-taught hedge-wizard. *If I'm lucky, whoever it is won't even have noticed the resonance-spell. And if he does—well, why shouldn't Master Edmond be looking over his new accommodations?*

Reassured, he cast the spell of silent unlocking. The young wizard sensed, rather than heard, the bolt slide open. He waited for a second, and then opened the door a bit and peered through the narrow gap. His view of the hall outside was blocked by a broad, armored back.

Randal eased the door shut, uncertain whether the emotion that gripped him was fear or contempt. Prince Vespian's laws against the use of magic in the city of Peda had done this much: Bartolomeo and his henchmen had no clear idea of how to deal with wizards. *They need more than bolts and guardsmen, if they don't want the hired help to run away.*

Randal paused a moment to draw breath, then cast the spell he'd been using to provide offstage sounds for Vincente and the other actors back in Peda. A second or so later, he was pleased to hear the noise of footsteps approaching, sounding like someone sneaking up around the corner.

The tap-tap of phantom heels on tile stopped just short of the corner. Randal listened for the sound of the guard going to investigate. He waited a moment longer, then cracked the door again. This time the guard's back no longer blocked his view.

Quickly, before the man could return from checking on the noise, Randal slipped out. By the time the guard returned, having found no one, the door was shut again, and Carvelli—or at least a fair imitation of him—stood waiting.

I think I got Carvelli's appearance right, Randal said to himself. *I hope the illusion of his voice works as well.* He did his best to put an arrogant snap in his tone as he looked down his nose at the guard. "When was the last time you polished that breastplate?"

The guard looked sheepish. "This morning, my lord, before I came on watch."

"See that you do it better next time."

"Yes, my lord," mumbled the guard.

Randal stalked off down the corridor. *That will give him something to think about,* he reflected, *so he won't remember he was ever away from his post.* Still wearing Carvelli's face, he retraced his steps to the room where he had left the unconscious man.

Two men guarded the outer doors. *My guess is that these fellows aren't paid to think, or to question what they see,* Randal thought. *If my disguise worked once, it'll work twice.* He strode up to the doors as if he owned the villa and all its contents. The man-at-arms on the right pulled one door open for him as he approached. Randal stepped through. The door clicked shut behind him.

The sound of voices brought him up short—from what Randal could hear, a heated argument was going on in the next room. He paused for a moment to listen. Maybe he could learn something useful.

"By thunder and death," said the voice of the real Carvelli, "I don't like it. I never liked the idea of bringing in an outsider, Your Grace, and I still don't."

Duke Bartolomeo's smoother voice answered, "We need him, Carvelli. While I appreciate all that you have done for me in the past, and will do in the future, we can't get inside my brother's defenses without using disguise—and that, you have told me, lies beyond your skill. Not only that, we need someone who can kill Petrucio. These things require a wizard. My brother knows as much. Why do you think he's banned all magic from the city?"

"If you must rely on purchased wizardry,"

persisted Carvelli, "you'd do well not to keep this Master Edmond alive beyond his usefulness."

"Nor will I," said Duke Bartolomeo. "But for now, we need him—and midnight approaches. It's time we started getting ready."

Footsteps approached the inner door. *I can't let them see me in here,* Randal thought. He pressed against the wall and cast a spell of invisibility on himself. *As long as I don't move, and they don't touch me . . .*

The door swung open. The real Carvelli and Duke Bartolomeo came out, followed by other men whom Randal didn't recognize. The Duke and his attendants passed out into the corridor, and the door crashed shut behind them.

With a sigh of relief, Randal dropped all the spells he'd been holding in place, except for his own earlier disguise as the mysterious Master Edmond. Then he walked over to where he'd hidden the man he'd been told to kill. The stranger lay motionless, but Randal saw that his bruises had already faded under the influence of the healing-spell.

I have to get him out of here, he thought. *Maybe he can tell me more about what's going on.*

Randal touched the man lightly, and the stranger's eyes opened. The young wizard clamped his hand across the man's mouth to stop him from talking. The gesture was needless; the man made no effort to speak.

Randal removed his hand. Laying a finger across his lips to warn the man to be silent, he stood up again and walked over to the outer door.

He listened a moment for sounds in the corridor. *Footsteps. Someone's coming.*

He moved quickly back toward the inner room where he had first met Duke Bartolomeo. No light showed, and Randal was certain the room was empty. He went in and gestured for the stranger to follow him.

Once they were both inside, Randal closed the door after them—and not a moment too soon. Footsteps sounded in the outer room. The young wizard and the man he had rescued flattened themselves against the wall.

Again, Randal cast invisibility over himself and his new companion. *I hope he knows not to move,* Randal thought.

A pale blue light shone around the edge of the door as it opened. Carvelli came in, the cold-flame glowing above one upraised hand. *So Carvelli is their hedge-magician. That's how he managed to search my room,* thought Randal. *But if he's been Schola-trained, then I'm the King of Elfland.*

Carvelli turned to Bartolomeo's desk and began shuffling through the papers that covered it. He scanned each sheet rapidly before casting it aside. And all the time he muttered, "Where is it? Where is it?"

At last, Carvelli found what he was looking for. He folded the piece of paper and stuffed it into the pouch at his belt. Then he froze.

Oh, no, Randal thought. *He suspects something.*

Carvelli stepped from beside the desk. He drew a dagger from his belt with his left hand, even as he

68

pulled his sword with his right. "Whoever is here, show yourself," Carvelli said in a low tone as he slowly circled the desk. He slashed the air in front of him, a whistling blow, then spun and slashed behind.

He knows someone invisible is here—he heard one of us breathing, perhaps—but he doesn't know who or where. And he doesn't know how invisibility works, either.

But Carvelli knew some tricks of his own. The hedge-wizard cast the cold-flame at the floor. The light formed a pool at his feet, then began to spread, slowly illuminating all the objects in the room. Randal knew that when the magical blue glow came to the two invisible watchers by the door, it would cover and outline them both.

Carvelli watched the spreading pool of blue light.

I could ambush him with a shock-spell, and he'd never have a chance, Randal thought. *But I haven't used any of the fighting-spells since Nick died in Widsegard, and I don't want to start now. If I have to, I'll cast a heat-spell on the metal of his sword's grip, so that he drops it, and then levitate him out the window.*

The pool of light reached Randal's feet and began to climb his legs. Randal didn't dare move his head to look down, lest the motion break the spell of invisibility all at once. But Carvelli saw him anyway.

"Caught you, spy," Carvelli hissed. "I was right not to trust you all along." He lunged, his sword's point aimed at Randal's heart. Randal jumped aside. The blade missed, ripping the wide sleeve of Randal's robe as it went by.

Carvelli recovered from the lunge and came back into line facing Randal. Randal knew that he

himself was no longer invisible—and the next lunge would strike true. *Now for the spell of heat,* he thought.

But he had scarcely framed the idea when the man he'd rescued stepped forward to a point just behind Carvelli and punched the hedge-wizard savagely in the back of the skull. The cold-flame vanished as Carvelli started to crumple. The other man caught him and lowered him to the floor without a sound.

"Did you have to do that?" Randal muttered. Almost automatically, he summoned up a cold-flame of his own to supply enough light to see by, now that Carvelli's was extinguished. "I had everything under control."

The other man was rummaging through the pouch at Carvelli's belt. He looked up as Randal spoke. "I don't know who you are, wizard—all I know is that you can't be who you're pretending to be. So why don't you stay out of my way?"

"You met me this morning," said Randal, speaking in a low tone so as not to alert the guards who waited just beyond the next room. "I'm Petrucio's journeyman. If you tell me what you're after, maybe I can help."

The man ignored him. "Aha. Got it." He pocketed the slip of paper.

"What's that?" Randal asked.

"The list of all the traitors in the palace. Now let's get out of here and back to Peda."

"You can't walk out of here looking like yourself," Randal pointed out. "You need a disguise."

The man nodded toward the unconscious Carvelli. "How about making me look like him?"

"I can do that." Randal looked again at the man he had rescued. "By the way, what's your name? I can't see spending the rest of the night saying 'Hey, you.'"

"You can call me Hernando," said the man, with a thin smile. "It's not my name, but it'll do."

"Well, then—stand still for a moment, Hernando, while I work the spell."

For a second time that evening, Randal created a magical likeness of the unconscious Carvelli. With the real Carvelli lying close at hand, and with the opportunity this time to observe and make corrections in his own work, the young wizard felt sure that this disguise was even better than the first time he'd tried it.

"There," he said, stepping back when he was done. "His own mother couldn't tell the difference now."

Hernando ignored his comment and bent over Carvelli's limp form. "Give me a hand tying this fellow up and stuffing him somewhere."

Together Randal and Hernando stripped Carvelli's stockings off his legs and used the fabric to bind the unconscious man's hands and feet. "I'll shove him under the desk," said Hernando, pulling the final knot tight as he spoke. "Can you do something to keep him there for a while?"

Randal nodded. "I'll put an invisibility-spell on him and a binding-spell on the knots. The invisibility won't lift until he moves, and he can't move until he manages to break the binding-spell. That should give us plenty of time to get past the guards and back to Peda."

The young wizard helped Hernando wrestle the bound and unconscious Carvelli into place under the desk, then spoke the words of invisibility and of binding over the henchman's unmoving form. Then Randal and Hernando—in the guise of Master Edmond and Carvelli—walked out of the suite and past the waiting guards.

Except for those guards, the hallway was deserted. Randal and Hernando went down that corridor, and then down others that were equally empty, always heading in the general direction of the villa's courtyard. Suddenly Randal stopped. He could hear voices and footsteps somewhere nearby—and growing nearer.

"We may have trouble," he said. "I don't think Master Edmond is supposed to be out of his room just yet."

Hernando wasted no time. "Quick," he said. "This way." The spy took Randal by the forearm and pulled him down a narrow side corridor, one plainly meant for the use of the duke's servants. After turning a couple of sharp corners, the passageway led straight to a dead end, closed off with a locked and barred door.

"Where are we now?" asked Randal.

"The dungeons," said Hernando.

"I didn't know Bartolomeo had any."

"He does. Can you open the door?"

Randal used the unlocking-spell. The door to the

villa's prison swung open. Hernando and the journeyman locked it again behind them.

They found themselves in a dim hallway with heavy barred and bolted doors at the far end. The only light came from moonlight slanting in through the windows of barred cells that opened off the long hall. All the cells were empty, except for the last. That cell contained a white-shirted form, lying on the straw that covered the floor.

As Randal and Hernando drew near, the prisoner stirred and looked up. Randal could barely conceal his surprise—it was Vincente. The actor was battered-looking and unshaven, but his bright red hair still proclaimed him unmistakably the same man with whom Randal had been rehearsing only last night.

Randal dropped his disguise as Master Edmond and stepped up to the iron grille that separated the cell from the hallway. "What on earth are you doing here, Vincente?" he asked.

"Someone caught me as I was walking home," the actor replied. "They pulled a sack over my head and carried me off. When the sack was removed, here I was—and here I've stayed ever since."

"How long have you been here?" Hernando asked.

"I'm not certain," Vincente told him. "But it's been two days, at least, since I arrived."

A cold feeling ran down Randal's spine. Two days? He had spoken with the actor only last evening. *If this is the real Vincente, then there's an imposter in the Prince's troupe.*

74

Then another, even colder feeling shivered through him: A key was turning at the far end of the corridor, where they had entered. Hastily, Randal cast the disguising-spell again—barely in time.

The door swung open. Into the pale silver moonlight stepped Bartolomeo, with bodyguards all around him.

VI.
Conspiracy

RELUCTANTLY, RANDAL MADE ready to throw a shock-spell. *I'll have to trust Hernando to open the far door while I hold off the guards,* he thought, *and I don't know* what *to do about poor Vincente.* . . .

But before he could act, Duke Bartolomeo broke the silence. "Ah, Carvelli," he said to Hernando. "I see you've fetched Master Edmond already. Good—let's start things moving."

The Duke turned to Randal. "How about it, wizard? Can you make me look like that man in the cell?"

Randal let the shock-spell fade away unused. "Easily, Your Grace," he said to Bartolomeo.

His words were true. The Duke and Vincente were already close to the same height and weight, and while Bartolomeo was a few years older than Prince Vespian's leading actor, the gap wasn't wide enough to give the young wizard any problems.

"I hope for all our sakes that you're right," said Bartolomeo. "This disguise must pass the inspection of my brother's wizard, Master Petrucio—and I'm told he has a great reputation in such matters."

"So he does," said Randal. "But what he doesn't suspect he won't look for."

Although if Petrucio doesn't suspect the worst already, Randal added to himself, *he certainly will after I've had a word or two alone with him.*

He kept his thoughts to himself. Raising his arms high in a theatrical gesture borrowed from the appearance of the ghost in tonight's performance, Randal began the conjuration to make the Duke look exactly like the imprisoned actor. He drew out the spell-working for as long as he could, making the magic a performance in its own right, as he shaped and colored the Duke's face and figure.

"*Fiat!*" he concluded. It was done. No one looking at the two men could have told the difference, except for the dirt and bruises on the face of the real Vincente.

Randal lowered his arms, hoping as he did so that nobody had noticed the unlocking-spell he'd worked on the cell door while he was creating the disguise. There wasn't much he could do for the actor without betraying himself, but he didn't like the idea of simply leaving him in Bartolomeo's power.

The Duke looked over at Hernando. "Well, Carvelli—do you still say we shouldn't have brought Master Edmond into our plans?"

Hernando shook his head. "No, my lord. The illusion is an excellent one. But how long will it hold?"

Randal suppressed a smile: The disguised spy was clearly worried about the durability of his own current appearance, as well as the Duke's. "It's good until I let it go," the young wizard said. "Like all such spells."

"Well, then," Bartolomeo said, "to the coaches, and away with us. We have great things to accomplish tonight."

The Duke turned, his long cloak flaring, and strode from the cell block. Randal and the others followed, leaving Vincente alone in the dark. *If he tries the door even once,* Randal thought as he made his way back through the villa with the rest of the Duke's henchmen, *he'll notice that the lock's been opened. Anything else will have to be up to him.*

In the courtyard, a pair of carriages waited. A footman opened the door of one for Bartolomeo, and the Duke climbed inside, motioning to Randal to come with him. The young wizard entered the carriage and looked over his shoulder in time to see the disguised Hernando climbing into the second carriage with another of the Duke's men.

The Duke reached up and rapped sharply with his knuckles on the roof of the carriage. The coachman's whip cracked once in response, and the carriage lurched forward.

This time the curtains were not drawn, and Randal could watch their progress across the countryside toward the city of Peda. As the carriage horses trotted on, the young wizard leaned back against the silk cushions and tried to look as though none of this was a mystery to him. Inwardly, however, his mind was awhirl with a multitude of confused guesses.

How much do I know, Randal asked himself, *and*

how much do I only suspect? Bartolomeo is planning to do something tonight during the performance, that much is certain . . . probably to kill Vespian, since he wants to make himself Prince in his brother's place.

Randal's thoughts raced on as he sat opposite the Duke in the swaying carriage. *How can I save the Prince? He's a good ruler, as far as I've seen, and this brother of his is a wicked man.*

"You're prepared to play your part, of course," Duke Bartolomeo began, breaking into Randal's thoughts. "But if you'll listen for a moment, I can offer you a reward far greater than what you were already promised."

The young wizard looked across at Bartolomeo, now perfectly disguised as the actor Vincente. *Why shouldn't I blast him as he sits?* Randal wondered. It took all his self-control to keep the temptation from showing on his face, despite the magical disguise he wore as Master Edmond. *I've known both the shock-spell and the lightning bolt-spell for years, and I've used them both against men before. Why do I hold my hand now?*

Randal sighed inwardly. He knew why he had been shrinking away from the powerful battle-magics, and the knowledge was no help at all. *I saw a friend die by magic. I don't know if I can ever bring myself to use spells like that again.*

"You'll still do what you've been hired for, of course," Bartolomeo went on, apparently taking Randal's silence for interest. "Disable the wizard Petrucio in whatever way seems best to you, but not before I stand before them all on the stage. When I

80

enter, make your move—then, and no sooner."

Randal nodded. "All that I agreed to, I will perform," he said. *And that's no lie,* he added to himself. *I promised this man nothing at all.* The thought brought him to the promises he had actually made. *The Prince doesn't want his brother harmed, and I can't change the decision for him on my own.*

"Good," said the Duke. Bartolomeo might be a cruel, cold man, Randal concluded, but the tension of the evening was loosening his tongue and making him talk to relieve his own nervousness. Now he looked at Randal and said, in a lower voice, "But say, will you stay on with me and be my court wizard? The gold I offered to you is still yours, regardless of your answer."

Randal didn't answer. *Let him think my silence is caution.*

The Duke went on after a brief pause. "Once Petrucio is dead, you will be the only wizard in Peda. Think of the power and wealth."

Bartolomeo leaned forward toward Randal and whispered, "And I need another service, in any case. I want you to kill Carvelli. I don't trust him—he'll be a threat to me as long as he's alive." The Duke leaned back and continued in louder tones, "And besides, who needs a self-taught conjurer when a Schola-trained wizard can have the honor?"

Randal felt sick. *This man betrays even his own people. I heard him promise Carvelli that I would be killed as soon as I'd performed my job.* He forced his voice to remain neutral. "Much remains to be done tonight, before we can speak of tomorrow, Your Grace," he said. "But this I promise: I will give you your answer when the Prince is dead."

"Call it done, then," the Duke said. "Dear brother Vespian will not see another dawn, and my blade will do the deed."

With another inward sigh, Randal turned away from Duke Bartolomeo and went back to looking out the window. *Prince Vespian doesn't want anyone to harm his brother. But if Petrucio and I fail, and the Prince dies . . . then what Vespian does or doesn't want isn't going to matter.*

And then the time for self-questioning was past. The carriage reached the palace gates—massive wrought-iron doors worked with the lion-and-dolphin device—and rattled up the long drive between ranks of armored guards.

Randal sank back against the cushions, trying to conceal a sudden feeling of dismay. None of the soldiers who stood guard looked like the ones he'd seen before, even though over the past weeks he'd come to recognize most of the palace men-at-arms. But he had recognized some of the liveried figures—they were the fighting men who had lounged around the courtyard of the Duke's villa. Whether Prince Vespian knew it or not, his brother Bartolomeo already held the palace.

The two carriages jolted to a halt before a lighted doorway. Before Randal could decide what to do, the carriage door opened, and the false Vincente stepped down and was gone.

Randal hesitated a moment. The man who had

ridden with Hernando in the second carriage walked up and spoke to him. "Come with me, Master Edmond. I'll take you to where you'll be standing."

The young wizard nodded, not trusting his voice. The two of them left the coach and walked through the palace doors into a lighted passage leading to the grand ballroom of Prince Vespian's palace. Inside the ballroom, music and laughter filled the air. Men and women in elegant clothing stood in the yellow radiance of countless wax candles.

The Midsummer Revels had indeed drawn guests from all over the known world—Randal spotted ambassadors from the surrounding city-states, as well as a plump Widsegardan merchant and one or two men in the flowing robes of the far east. Master Petrucio, however, was nowhere in sight, and neither was Prince Vespian.

Then Randal heard Lys's familiar alto voice singing at the far end of the ballroom, and he smiled. Lys would be able to come and go unhindered. *She'll be able to get word to Petrucio backstage,* he thought, *even if I'm not able to slip away long enough to do it myself.*

He hurried off through the crowded ballroom, heading for the music, but when he reached his goal, he frowned. Lys was there, all right, dressed in a fine gown of black and silver, and playing on a new lute with exquisite sweetness. But she was seated up above in the musicians' gallery, where Randal couldn't reach her.

Still frowning, he stood looking upward for a

moment. *How do I let her know that I'm here?*

Then the answer came to him. Just as he had done so many times before, in market squares across Occitania, he set up a magical chord below her own music, then layered on melody and harmony to make a moving tapestry of sound.

Lys looked down at the crowd below the musicians' gallery with a surprised expression on her face. But, polished entertainer that she was, she didn't miss a beat or sing a false note. Instead, she switched effortlessly into another song, the same tune they had used to entertain the crowds as they worked their way from Widsegard to Occitania.

She knows I've come back, Randal thought with satisfaction. *But how can I tell her where to find me, without alerting the entire hall?*

He glanced back up at the balcony and bit his lip in irritation. Lys had vanished while Randal was thinking about the problem, and now a quartet of musicians stood in her place. Behind the performers, a tall, red-haired man stood watching.

Vincente.

No, Randal reminded himself. *Duke Bartolomeo. I have to get away and tell Petrucio what's going on. The Prince mustn't attend the performance tonight.*

Randal stole a quick look around the room. He noticed with relief that the nearest doorway was an inconspicuous one leading back into the servants' and actors' quarters. As he looked down the passage, he saw a tall, red-haired form walk across the hall and disappear down an intersecting corridor.

Vincente again.

Randal doubted his eyes for a moment. Perhaps it had been one of the palace messengers. Then he shook his head. No, he was sure. It had been the actor. Then he looked back to the balcony.

Vincente stood there, just as before.

One of them must be the real one, thought Randal. *Or else it's the imposter in the troupe. But why would that one be here, if his master Duke Bartolomeo has taken his place . . . and if he doesn't work for Bartolomeo, then where does his loyalty lie?*

Now the young wizard knew that simply passing a warning through Lys wouldn't be good enough. Things had gotten too complicated for that. He had to tell Petrucio everything—and soon, before matters really got out of hand. He started toward the guard blocking the passage out of the ballroom.

I have to get past him somehow without being noticed, Randal thought. *It's too bad invisibility doesn't work on a moving object.*

He considered using another disguise-spell. *No, that won't work either. People would notice the change. Besides, I'm keeping up three disguises already. That's not my limit, but it's close.*

Randal shook his head. *I'm a journeyman wizard; I should be able to slip out of a room full of people without being seen.*

Just as he was about to give up, he suddenly recalled the actor Vincente's own words from that interrupted rehearsal of a week or so ago: "Just give us a flash of light and a loud bang, and it'll cover anything awkward."

I've got it! Randal thought, smiling to himself. He

started off toward the guarded doorway. When he was only a pace or so away, he cast the spell he'd been preparing as he walked.

Without warning, the bracket of candles nearest the guard blazed up in a flare of brilliant light. All eyes—including the guard's—turned to the flash of blue and yellow fire, as all ten of the candles burned down to their holders at once. In that moment, Randal took three quick paces past the guard and into the hallway, then started running.

Nobody followed him. *When all this is over,* he thought, *I'll have to thank Vincente for giving me the idea I needed.*

He ducked down passages at random for a while, and then began to work his way toward Petrucio's study. *Maybe he's still there waiting for me—I didn't see him in the crowd back in the ballroom. If he isn't, at least I can try to find the Prince from there.*

As he hurried through the palace corridors, he heard in the distance the sound of a giant gong being struck, and a herald crying, "All are invited to the theatre, to join His Grace, Prince Vespian the Magnificent, Sovereign Ruler of Peda, in viewing the Midsummer Night's performance of *The Nephew's Revenge!*"

The young wizard ran even faster, afraid that a worse tragedy was about to befall the Prince than had ever been acted for him by his players.

VII.
Masks

THE DOOR TO Petrucio's study was closed when Randal got there, but yellow light showed around the edges. *Good,* thought Randal. *He's still working.* He turned the knob and entered without knocking.

"Master Petrucio!" he called out as he stepped over the threshold. "Master Petrucio!"

"Stand right there, you," said a low female voice. Randal turned toward the sound and saw Lys, already dressed in her costume for the play. The light from a many-branched candlestick glittered off the silver threads in her brocaded gown—and off the knife she held at the ready in her hand.

"I don't know who you are," she said, "but you shouldn't have been able to open the door like that."

"Lys," said Randal. "You can put away the knife. It's me."

"Randy?" Lys's blue eyes looked puzzled.

That's right, Randal thought. *I still look like Master Edmond.*

"I should have left you back in Tarnsberg," he said

in the language of Brecelande, and let the illusion lapse.

Lys lowered the knife and smiled. "It *is* you!"

"That's right," said Randal. With his own disguise gone, he felt less fatigued, although he could still sense the disguises on Hernando and Bartolomeo draining at his powers. "But what are you doing here? The play's about to start."

"I know," she said. "Master Petrucio is covering for you at the theatre. He told me to meet you here when you showed up—the door would let me in and out, he said, but you were the only other person it would open for. I think Petrucio was worried about you."

"So was I," said Randal. "Did he give you a message?"

Lys nodded. "He said that things were changing too fast to give you any directions, and you should do as you think best."

"That's all?" Randal asked in disappointment. He'd hoped that when he found the master wizard he could hand him the entire confusing problem. "Duke Bartolomeo is trying to kill the Prince, and somebody has to stop him."

Lys put away her knife. "Then let's get back to the theatre."

Randal extinguished the candles with a puff of magical breeze, and then he and Lys headed back out into the palace corridors. They reached the players' entrance to the theatre, and Randal paused. "You can look for Petrucio backstage," he said. "Tell him to stop Vincente any way he can."

"Vincente? But what's he—"

"I'll explain later," said Randal hurriedly. "I'd better go around to the front to warn the Prince."

Before mingling back among Bartolomeo's men, he cast the disguise-spell on himself again—the appearance of Master Edmond was becoming easier and easier to slip into each time he made the change. Then he started down the hall. When he got close to the main entrance of the Prince's theatre, Randal slowed to a pace more befitting a gray-haired wizard of Master Edmond's years and walked unquestioned past the guards at the door.

Inside the theatre, Prince Vespian's guests packed the ranks of cushioned benches. From where Randal stood at the back of the room, he could see the Prince sitting in the center of the front row—the ruler's massive throne rose up out of the low benches like a wooden mountain. Master Petrucio sat in the row behind the Prince, just a few feet away from him.

I've got to warn them, thought Randal. He began edging along the side of the room, making his way toward the Prince a row or so at a time. He hadn't gone far when a hand fell on his shoulder. He turned and recognized the man who had escorted him from Bartolomeo's carriage into the palace.

"Thank goodness you're here!" said the Duke's henchman. "I thought I'd lost you. Hurry up and get into position—if Vespian's wizard isn't taken care of, our endeavor will be over before it even starts, and so much for all our hopes."

He took Randal by the elbow and pushed him

farther forward, until the young wizard was standing against the wall in a spot directly in line with where Master Petrucio sat. *So close,* thought Randal. *But he doesn't know I'm here. If I call out, Bartolomeo's man will probably kill me . . . unless I take care of that one first.*

Randal slowly clenched his right hand into a fist. His disguise as Master Edmond hid the long scar across his palm, but he could feel the old wound aching with the gesture. *This is no quarrel of mine,* he thought. *I could still walk out of here and let these southerners fight each other without my help.*

But Master Petrucio had trusted him. . . . The young wizard sighed and began to make ready the spells that would render the Duke's henchman unconscious and allow Randal to defend himself against Bartolomeo's other followers in the theatre long enough to call out his message. Then he had another idea. *I can use the spell of magical resonance instead,* he thought, with relief. *Petrucio has to notice it—he'll know that it's me.*

Randal cast the resonance-spell. As he'd expected, magical power came back at him from several sources. Randal could sense a number of minor charms at work on the stage and in the wings—the actors' disguises and the illusory effects for the first act. *Petrucio's covering for me like he said he would.*

Over and beyond the lesser magics, the master wizard's power echoed back at the journeyman like silent thunder. But as the effects of the resonance-spell died away, Randal frowned. He'd purposely directed most of the spell's force toward the spot where Master Petrucio sat, only a few paces away from the Prince—but the dark-haired figure in the cloth-of-gold robes had no feeling of magic about it at all.

Illusion? Randal wondered. He thought of casting the spell of true seeing, but an elbow jabbed into his ribs before he could act.

"Make yourself ready now, Master Edmond," whispered the conspirator. "And look to the stage."

Randal looked, in time to see a pale and distracted-seeming Lys turn to stage left and deliver the line that heralded Vincente's first entrance as the Nephew:

"But who is this who walks the house by night?"

Promptly on cue, Vincente—no, Randal reminded himself, Bartolomeo—strode from the wings onto the stage. Bartolomeo's likeness to the red-haired actor was exact, but with a closer look, Randal was able to detect the lingering traces of his own magic clinging to the disguise. The Duke wore the black-and-silver costume Vincente had chosen for the Nephew as a compliment to the Prince, and carried the Nephew's drawn sword in his hand.

As Randal watched, Bartolomeo strode forward to the front of the stage, as if to deliver the first soliloquy—only to cry out in a loud voice, "Happy Midsummer, brother!" and leap down to drive his sword-point through Vespian's body.

In the same moment, Master Petrucio, or the illusion of him, vanished completely. Bartolomeo

91

pulled out his bloodied sword and ran back up the steps at the side of the stage.

"People of Peda!" he shouted.

The men and women in the audience had rushed forward toward the slumping figure of the wounded Prince. At the sound of Bartolomeo's voice, they halted—and then drew back gasping as another figure in black and silver ran out of the wings with sword in hand.

Vincente!

"Coward!" the actor shouted, in a voice that carried to the balconies. "Killer of unarmed men! Fight *me!*"

Bartolomeo turned, his sword-point red. Blades clashed as the two Vincentes faced one another across naked steel.

The Duke's henchman was babbling in Randal's ear—something about "doing a good job there with Vespian's wizard"—but Randal barely heard him. The young wizard was too busy casting the spell of magical resonance again, in a desperate attempt to find the vanished Petrucio. But once more he failed to locate the older wizard. Worse, the sense of Petrucio's magic had weakened and started to fade.

I've got to get to the Prince, Randal thought. *If I don't work the healing-spells soon, he's going to die . . . and a wound like that isn't something I can handle from across the room.* He looked at the frightened audience, some of them pressing forward toward the front row, others struggling to escape out the rear of the theatre, where guardsmen turned them back. The uproar was deafening. *I'll never make it through all these people.*

92

Randal glanced at the Duke's henchman. His attention was focused on the two swordsmen, Duke and actor, fighting on the stage. *Time to do my vanishing act again,* Randal thought, and ran out the back of the theatre.

A guard moved as if to stop him, lowering a halberd across the doorway. Randal snapped, "The Duke's business!" and pushed the halberd aside.

Then he was out in the hallway and running.

The stairway to the prop-loft was nearby, off a turn in the corridor. Randal found the door, unlocked it with a quick spell, and started climbing the staircase.

At the top, the stairs opened into a wide, flat area with a trap door in the center. Randal lifted the trap door and found himself looking down onto the stage from above.

The play had broken off in mid-scene with Bartolomeo's entrance, and the actors had scattered into the wings, but directly below Randal, Bartolomeo and Vincente still fought to and fro across the boards. Another time, Randal might have been amused by their style of fighting—all thrust and parry, with none of the long, arcing edge-cuts that enabled the heavier swords of Brecelande to cut through chain mail and leather—but now his eyes were fixed on the men themselves.

I saw this, too, in my vision. Identical men, struggling, with Petrucio trapped between them.

"How much," he heard one Vincente say to the other as their sword-blades met and parted, "how much—do I have to pay you—to lay down your sword?"

"Assassin!" snarled the other Vincente, as he lunged again. "Keep your—blasted money!"

The fight went on. Beyond the two swordsmen, Randal saw Vespian slumped, bleeding, in his chair. One of the Prince's courtiers was trying to stop the flow of red with what looked like a lace-trimmed handkerchief. A few feet away, the disguised Hernando was pushing his way toward the Prince through the crowd of spectators.

He's going to need some help, thought Randal. *He'll never be able to get Prince Vespian out of there alone.*

He looked about the crowded prop-loft. A coil of rope hung from a peg nearby. Randal took it and made one end fast to a beam that supported the roof overhead.

He paused for a moment on the lip of the trap door. *I'd better look like myself again,* he decided. *Bartolomeo's people don't know who I really am, and this way, "Master Edmond" won't be seen helping the Prince.*

With a word, he dispelled the illusory features of Bartolomeo's hired wizard and resumed his own appearance. Then he tossed down the rope. Before it fell completely, Randal wrapped the heavy sleeves of his journeyman's robe around his hands. He grasped the rope through the cloth and launched himself into space, sliding down onto the stage below.

Lys ran out to him from the wings as soon as his feet hit the boards. "Randy—you have to heal the Prince!"

"I'm trying to get to him," Randal said. "But everybody's in the way!"

He gestured at the strip of stage between the two of them and Prince Vespian. Back and forth across that space, the two Vincentes fought on, so deep in their combat that they didn't notice Randal's arrival.

"Come with me," said Lys. She ran back off into the wings, and Randal went after her in time to see her lifting up a trap door like the one overhead. She dropped down through it, and Randal followed.

"We keep props and supplies down here," he heard her say, in a calmer voice, "and there's another door under the front of the stage. You remember—they brought the benches out through it yesterday evening." And then, "Oh, no. The storeroom door's locked from the outside."

"Let me," Randal said, as he cast yet another in what felt like the longest series of unlocking-spells he'd ever cast. He heard a clank as the outer bolt moved aside, and then he and Lys pushed the door open. From under the stage, they could see the Prince sagging in his throne, the blood still flowing from the wound in his shoulder.

"Close your eyes," Randal said to Lys. He threw a ball of brilliant light into the air, strong enough to dazzle the onlookers, and then ran out of his hiding place before anyone could recover. He grabbed the Prince, pulling him from his seat, and half-dragged, half-carried the bigger man back to the stage-front.

"Grab his legs!" he called to Lys. He pushed Vespian's limp body through and scrambled back into the storage space after it, swinging the door shut behind him.

It was dark in the storage room under the stage.

Randal summoned up a sphere of cold-flame and looked down at Prince Vespian by its chilly, blue-white light.

The ruler of Peda was in a bad way. Blood matted the black velvet of his tunic, and more of the dark fluid flowed from the wound in his shoulder. His dark features had gone pale, reminding Randal of how his cousin Walter had looked after the demon-fight in Master Balpesh's tower, when the young knight had lain near death from his wounds.

"Is it too late?" asked Lys. "Can you still help him?"

"I hope so," said Randal. Most wizards scorned healing-spells as work that any untaught healwife or country shepherd could do as well—but Randal had learned the spells from a master wizard who had made them his particular study.

Lys bent closer to the wounded Prince, and then looked up at Randal. "He's trying to say something," she said. "But I can't understand him."

Randal halted his preparations. Lys was right—the Prince was muttering a continuous stream of words. The young wizard leaned forward to listen.

It's no wonder Lys can't understand him, Randal thought in astonishment. The young wizard looked up at Lys. "He's talking in the Old Tongue."

"Can you tell what he's saying?"

Randal nodded. "It's a continuation-spell—it makes other spells permanent, so that they can stay in place after the death of the wizard who cast them."

"But Prince Vespian isn't a wizard!" protested Lys.

"No, he isn't," said Randal. He spoke the words that would dispel illusion and caught his breath as the magic took effect. The man who lay bleeding on the floor was the master wizard, Petrucio.

"Master Petrucio!" Randal cried. "What are you doing here? And where is the Prince?"

The master wizard gave no answer, but kept on muttering the words of his conjuration. "*Fiat!*" he ended, and drew a long, gasping breath. He let it out in a sigh. "The spell is done—and so am I, I think."

"You're not going to die," Randal said. "I'm going to heal you. But tell me first, quickly—where's the Prince, and what's going on?"

"Ah, Randal," whispered Petrucio. "I thought it was you." His eyes opened and focused on the young journeyman. "Bartolomeo is trying to kill the Prince—I didn't expect—"

The master wizard's eyelids started to flutter and close again, and Randal said urgently, "The Prince— Master Petrucio, where is the Prince?"

"Vespian?" Petrucio's voice was fading. "Where he always is, in the . . ." The words trailed off into silence.

VIII.
The Prince's Friends

"HURRY, RANDY!" exclaimed Lys. "He's almost gone."

Randal was already speaking the words of strength and wholeness. Petrucio's breathing slowed and steadied, and the blood stopped trickling down his chest as the wound closed over. Soon the master wizard lay deep in a healing sleep.

Randal sat back against one of the thick wooden pillars that supported the stage from underneath. His own breath came ragged and heavy for a few moments. Casting a healing-spell always tired him, and now he had done it twice in one day, once for Hernando and once for Petrucio.

Overhead, the stage floor vibrated with the noise of the sword fight going on above, where Vincente— or his double—still held the Duke locked in single combat. Randal was tempted to rest in the dark storeroom for a while longer, but he forced himself back onto his feet.

Whether he knows it or not, and wherever his true loyalties may lie, Vincente is buying us time. We can't afford to waste any of it.

Lys had followed Randal's upward glance. When he stood, she rose to her feet, as well. "What do we do now?" she asked.

"We save the Prince," Randal told her. "Or we try to, anyway. Wherever he is."

He heard her give a faint sigh. "Before we go any further, let me see if I have this straight. You really are Randal of Doun, and not some other wizard who happens to look like him for the moment. Right so far?"

Randal nodded.

Lys crossed her arms on her chest. "Then you have to be the same Randal of Doun who swore last night at rehearsal that he'd given up trying to cure the world's problems. Are you sure you know what you're doing?"

"I'm me, and you're Lys, and this man lying here is Master Petrucio. And that," Randal concluded in weary tones, "is about *all* that I'm sure of. But I've taken the Prince's hospitality, and I can't stand by and see him murdered."

"You picked a fine time to get back your sense of duty," Lys told him. She looked at him for a moment in the glow of the witchlight. "So you're going out there. What then?"

"Find the Prince," said Randal. "And save him, if I can." He glanced down at the motionless form of Master Petrucio, still deeply asleep on the dusty floor of the under-stage, and then he looked back at

100

Lys. "You'll be safe down here. I'll put a locking-spell on all the entrances as I go out, just in case. Master Petrucio should be able to break it easily enough once he recovers, but I don't think anybody else in Peda is that good."

Lys was already shaking her head. "I'm not going to stay idle down here in the dark while you're up there trying to get yourself killed."

"Killing a wizard is harder than it looks," said Randal. "But we don't have time to argue. Come on, then."

The young wizard retraced his way to the trap door that led up into the wings of the stage and flung it open. He climbed out as fast as he could, with Lys following. As soon as she was clear, he slammed down the trap door and cast the locking-spells. *At least Master Petrucio is safe,* he thought, and turned his attention to the theatre.

From where Randal and Lys stood in the wings, they could tell that nothing had changed for the better. Vincente and Bartolomeo still fought up and down the front of the stage—seeing them together, Randal could pick out the Duke by the disguise-spell covering him. *But when I concentrate, there's something about Vincente that feels funny, too. . . . I wish I knew what it was.*

Out beyond the stage, people no longer crowded around Vespian's throne as they had a few minutes before. Men-at-arms in black and silver lined the walls of the theatre and blocked its entrance. Some of the guards carried heavy crossbows, with short, stubby bolts already laid in place and ready to shoot.

101

A crossbow bolt could go through metal: Randal didn't blame the silk and velvet–clad audience for keeping still.

So far, though, the guards hadn't interfered with the duel onstage, where Vincente and the disguised Bartolomeo were engaged in a precise and deadly passage of arms. Identically booted feet stamped on the wooden stage as the two men lunged back and forth, and the slender blades of their swords clicked as the weapons met and parted. Guards and audience alike watched as if held in place by a powerful spell. *It's fear,* Randal realized, *fear that's holding them. Nobody can tell the two Vincentes apart, and nobody wants to chance shooting the wrong man.*

Suddenly the duelists separated and stood for a moment as if frozen, with their blades still crossed near the tips. Bartolomeo and Vincente seemed as closely matched in skill and speed as if they had been twins in truth, and Randal knew that in that motionless silence each man would be watching the other—looking for that first hint of flinching or hesitation that would provide an opening.

Then a third slender, red-headed figure sprang out of the wings, on the side opposite Randal and Lys, and joined the two duelists in the center of the stage.

Vincente.

The *real* Vincente, Randal was sure of it—this one was Bartolomeo's kidnapped original, still wearing the black hose and loose white shirt he'd worn in the cell at the villa. Like his two duplicates, the actor held a sword in his hand. *But if* that's *Vincente,* Randal thought, *and one of the others is Bartolomeo,*

102

then who's the third one—and which side is he really on?

The newcomer swept his blade down onto the crossed swords of the duelists in a stroke that beat all three blades point downward toward the floor. In ringing tones, he declaimed the opening words from Act Two of *The Nephew's Revenge:*

"So, brothers, we are met again!"

Bartolomeo spat out a curse. With a little concentration, Randal could see through his disguise and discern the Duke's features beneath.

But to Randal's surprise, the other black-and-silver Vincente laughed aloud as he stepped back into the guard position. "Well met, indeed, my brother!" he called out—the next line of the play, and one that made the actor laugh in his turn. As if on an unspoken signal, the two men turned together to threaten Bartolomeo.

The Duke stepped back, and Randal saw his eyes go to the crossbowmen lining the walls of the theatre.

No, you don't! thought Randal.

Before anyone could give the order to shoot, the young wizard summoned up a blast of magical wind. The wind blew down the length of the theatre like the first gust of a blizzard, and all the candles extinguished themselves as one. Darkness filled the room, and a woman screamed. Randal heard the thrumming noise of a single released bowstring, and the solid *chunk!* of a crossbow bolt burying itself in wood.

With a smell like burning string, the spluttering

candles lit themselves again. *Who did that?* wondered Randal. *It wasn't me, and Petrucio would never be so clumsy.*

A quick motion out in the audience caught the young wizard's eye. It was Carvelli—not the disguised Hernando; *that* man was pushing his way toward the nearest side door, with the expression of one who wasn't going to let a mere guard halt his escape. The Carvelli who stood framed in the theatre's rear entrance was the genuine article, the Duke's hedge-wizard whom Hernando had stunned and left behind in Bartolomeo's villa.

"My Lord Bartolomeo!" he shouted, from the back of the theatre. "My Lord Bartolomeo! Treason!"

But the disguised Bartolomeo was gone; only the other two Vincentes remained. As Randal watched, the two men—one in black and silver, one in a prison-stained white shirt and plain black hose—exchanged glances and ran offstage.

"Where are they going?" Lys exclaimed at Randal's elbow.

"I don't know . . ." began Randal, and then all his memories of the palace clicked together. "Secret door," he said. "There has to be a door backstage to the secret passage."

"Can you find it by magic?" she asked.

"Not fast, but I can try—no, wait. Master Petrucio's study!" Once more he invoked the disguise-spell and assumed the form of Master Edmond, Duke Bartolomeo's hired wizard. "Let's hope the guards at the actors' entrance still think I'm on their side. Come on."

Luck was with them; a curt "Duke's business" got them past the guards and out into the hall. As soon as Randal and Lys were out of sight around the first corner, the young wizard changed back to his own appearance. Then he started off at a run through the narrow corridors of the servants' wing, with Lys following behind as fast as her long skirts would allow.

She caught up with him while he was opening the door to Petrucio's study. "Now I remember why I always liked short tunics and stockings for the road," she said ruefully. "There's enough cloth in this gown to make a tent."

The door to the room swung open as she spoke. Randal hurried across to the panel that hid the secret door and slid it aside. "From here we can get to the Prince's private apartments," he said over his shoulder to Lys. "If we find Vespian alive anywhere, it'll be there."

"Then what are we waiting for?" Lys stepped past him into the dark mouth of the entrance. Then she drew back again, almost bumping into him in her haste. "Listen!" she exclaimed. "What's that noise?"

Randal froze. Now he, too, could hear a sound that had become familiar to him during the past hour—the clash and whisper of a pair of thin, sharp Pedan swords striking and sliding against one another.

"They're coming this way," he said. "Let's get back out into the hall."

Together, they retreated to the far side of the hallway. "Don't move," murmured Randal as soon as he felt the cool wood of the paneled wall at his back. "I'm going to make us invisible. I want to see what's going on."

He said the words of the spell—and barely in time. The clashing of metal on metal grew louder. Within the darkened workroom, a pair of shadowy figures emerged from the open door of the secret passage. Faint candlelight slanted in from the hallway and glinted off the blades of their swords as they fought.

The two figures were identical in size and height, but Randal could tell them apart by their clothing, even from where he stood. One man wore black and silver, making him a darker patch of shadow where metallic threads picked up the light and glittered like distant stars. The loose white shirt of the second man was a pale, moving blob in the dimness as he parried his opponent's thrusts.

That one's Vincente, Randal thought. *The Vincente I freed from the cell at the Duke's villa, anyway. So the other must be Bartolomeo himself.*

A moment's concentration confirmed his guess— the disguise-spell he had wrought for the Duke was still in place. The other man must have overtaken Bartolomeo somewhere in the secret passage and tried to stop him. But before Randal could act to stop Bartolomeo and bring an end to the fight, the Duke lunged and put his sword through his enemy's body.

The other man fell bleeding to the floor. The Duke stood looking at his former opponent for the space of a few heartbeats. "You were clever," he said, "but you came too late. As for your twin, whoever he really is—I'll serve him as I did my own, once Peda is mine."

He bent down and wiped the blood off his sword with the tail of the man's shirt, then stepped back through the open entrance of the secret passage and vanished into the dark.

Randal dropped the invisibility-spell as soon as he dared and ran into the workroom with Lys close at his heels. He struck up the cold-flame, filling the chamber with pale blue light, and knelt over Vincente's body.

Blood still flowed from the man's wound, spreading out over the white linen shirt in a dark, ugly stain. Lys knelt down opposite Randal. In the witchlight, her face looked unhappy and bleached of color.

"Is he dead?" she asked.

"No," said Randal. "The wound isn't a mortal one—I can heal him." He laughed briefly, without mirth. "If Bartolomeo had been the type to make certain, instead of making speeches, the story might be different."

"Heal him if you can," said a voice from the hallway behind them—Vincente's voice, grown familiar to both of them through the long hours of rehearsal. Randal looked around quickly and saw that the speaker was indeed the Vincente in black and silver, the one who had first challenged Bartolomeo while Petrucio lay stricken. Now the newcomer took a step forward to gaze at the bloodied figure of his double.

"Here's another one who has paid dearly tonight

for his loyalty," said the man in black and silver. "Do your best for him—but hurry. I know where the Duke will be going."

Randal nodded and worked a spell to close the wound and keep the injured man safely asleep until help could come. *Thank goodness he wasn't hurt as badly as Master Petrucio. This makes the third healing I've done today.*

When the work was finished, Randal rose to his feet, swaying a little with momentary dizziness. The man in black and silver caught him by the arm and steadied him. "Neatly done," he said to the young wizard. "Now let's be off."

"Wait a minute." It was Lys who spoke, standing on the threshold of the secret passage with her knife once more in her hand. "Just who *are* you, anyway?"

"The same Vincente you've always known, Demoiselle Lys," said the man with a courtly bow. "And a true friend of the Prince—which is more important now, I think." He stepped past her without another word, ignoring the knife as if it didn't exist, and became a shadow moving swiftly off into the darkness.

Randal and Lys hurried after him, with the cold-flame lighting their way. Several minutes later, the man ahead paused, pushed aside a sliding panel, and stepped out of the passage into a darkened room. Randal and Lys followed.

By the light of the cold-flame, Randal saw that the room contained a simple bed and rows of bookshelves. The man in black and silver—*call him Vincente,* Randal thought, *since he seems to think he's got a right to the name*—closed the panel and motioned Randal and Lys forward to the double doors on the other side of the room.

Vincente put his eye to the crack where the two doors met, peered through, and shook his head. "He's here already," he said. "That's going to make things a bit harder."

Curious, Randal bent and looked through the keyhole of one door into the adjoining room. The narrow view wasn't the best he could have asked for, but he glimpsed enough of the next room to recognize the royal apartments he had seen that morning—or was it yesterday morning by now?—when he had accompanied Master Petrucio to his audience with the Prince.

There was a man seated at the Prince's desk. But it wasn't the Prince. The seated figure moved, putting his booted feet up on the desk and leaning back in a comfortable position. Now Randal recognized him—Duke Bartolomeo's hedge-wizard, Lord Carvelli.

A door opened in the far wall beyond the desk, and Duke Bartolomeo—still disguised as Vincente—stepped into the room. Carvelli swung to his feet.

"Which one are you?" the hedge-wizard asked.

Bartolomeo gave a triumphant laugh. "You know me, Carvelli. Vespian is dead by my hand—and I am the rightful ruler of Peda!"

IX.
Sword Dance

RANDAL SQUINTED THROUGH the keyhole at the two men in the next room. With his view so limited, and both the Duke and Carvelli moving in and out of sight, it was hard to tell reality from illusion without casting a spell of magical resonance. He closed both eyes and concentrated instead on the feel of magic in the air.

"Wait a minute," he murmured, as much to himself as to Vincente and Lys. "That's not Carvelli, that's Hernando."

"Who?" whispered the others, as one voice.

"One of Petrucio's men," said Randal. "He's on our side."

In the other room, Bartolomeo strode up and down, gesturing grandly with the sword he still carried in his right hand. "*I* rule now, Carvelli. Fetch Master Edmond, so that I can regain my true face and form."

Randal saw the disguised Hernando hesitate. Bartolomeo lifted the tip of his sword slightly and pointed with it toward the door. "Make haste,

Carvelli. My loyal subjects await me in the theatre."

In the darkened inner chamber, the man called Vincente touched Randal on the arm. "This Master Edmond," said the older man, low-voiced. "Do you know him well enough to put on his face?"

"Yes," said Randal, biting back a smile. "I do."

"Good. Go back into the passage and turn left— you'll find another door opening out through a fireplace."

Randal nodded, remembering his journey through the secret passage with Petrucio the morning before. "I know the door you're talking about."

"Then let the Duke's henchman find Master Edmond there," Vincente continued. "The sooner Bartolomeo puts on his true face, the sooner we can begin to work our way out of this tangle."

Randal gave another nod and ducked back into the passageway, assuming the guise of Master Edmond as he went. He came out through the fireplace in time to watch Hernando striding past him toward the doors at the far end of the long room. Randal stepped away from the hearth and cleared his throat.

Hernando turned. "It's about time you showed up again," the spy growled in an angry whisper. "Bartolomeo's won, thanks to you—if you'd been doing your job, Vespian wouldn't be dead."

"He's not dead," said Randal. "I still don't know where the Prince is, but I know Bartolomeo got the wrong man."

Hernando drew a sharp breath through his teeth.

112

"Then the game may not be lost . . . at least not yet. Come on, let's play it out to the end."

The disguised agent turned and headed back into the royal apartments with Randal following close behind him. They walked through the doors surmounted with the lion-and-dolphin ornamentation, into the room where Randal had met Vespian the day before. This time, however, it was Bartolomeo who waited, still wearing the actor Vincente's face.

The Duke smiled as Randal entered. "Now then, Master Edmond, we are met in much happier circumstances. Only undo what you did before, and the evening will be ours."

"Easily done, Your Grace," said Randal, suiting the action to his words. The disguise fell away from Bartolomeo, revealing once more the Duke's true features—so like, and so unlike, those of the Prince. "You are yourself again."

"Our thanks, Master Edmond," said the Duke. "In days to come, you will find us suitably grateful. In the meantime . . ." Bartolomeo reached into his brother's desk and pulled out a handful of gold coins. "Consider this a partial payment for services already rendered."

Randal shook his head. "We can settle accounts later, Your Grace."

"Very well," said Bartolomeo. He pocketed the coins and turned to the disguised Hernando. "Come, Carvelli—it's time we presented ourselves at the theatre."

Bartolomeo strode out of the Prince's study, with

the disguised Hernando close on his heels. Randal waited for a few moments, until he was sure the two men were out of earshot, and then looked at the doors leading to the bedchamber.

"Lys?" he called softly. "Vincente?"

The doors opened, and the others emerged. The man who called himself Vincente had a tenseness about him that Randal hadn't noticed before.

"So the usurper has his own face again," Vincente said. He turned to Randal and Lys. "Now to see who in the palace is loyal and who is not. Are you with me?"

"Where are we going?" Lys asked.

Vincente gave a brief laugh. "Where else should actors go but to the theatre? Most of the guests will prove true to Vespian, I think—if they believe they have some choice besides Duke Bartolomeo or chaos."

The actor stepped through the secret door and beckoned to Randal and Lys to follow. Once again, his shadowy black-and-silver figure led them rapidly along the hidden passage. Some of the narrow, tunnel-like corridor Randal remembered from the day before, when he had come to the Prince's quarters with Master Petrucio, but the rest of it was unfamiliar. Vincente, however, seemed to find his way without pausing to think.

"You certainly know your way around the palace," Randal observed as they half-walked, half-ran down a cramped and sloping hallway that was lightless except for the glow of Randal's cold-flame.

"I was born and raised here," Vincente said.

114

"Secret passages make wonderful hiding places for a small boy. By the time I grew up and joined the Prince's players, I knew as much about His Grace's palace as he did himself." Once again, the actor laughed. "I never suspected my old pranks would turn out to be useful someday—and here we are."

"Where's here?" asked Lys. The passage had narrowed to a dead end where the three of them stood facing a closed door set into a brick wall. "This place has more secret doorways than a cheese has holes."

"We're inside the archway over the front of the stage," Vincente told her. "On stage right it's solid masonry, but this side is hollow. Bartolomeo escaped through here when the candles went out—whose doing was that, anyway?"

"Mine," admitted Randal. "He was about to order his crossbowmen to shoot."

"Reckless of him," said Vincente. "But typical. Most of the other guards are still loyal to the Prince, I think—they've just been given bad orders. Once things have settled down, the Prince can sort out the confused ones from the turncoats easily enough."

"What makes *you* so sure the Prince is alive?" Lys asked.

"Call it a hunch," said Vincente. The actor turned to the door and opened it a crack. He looked out through the tiny opening, nodded to himself with an expression of satisfaction, and turned back to the others. "Randal—put one of your disguise-spells on me, to make me look like Vespian, and together we can end this farce."

Randal thought back to the healing-spell he'd worked in the theatre the morning before, and how Vincente had spoken to him then of being a power in the state. "If I help you," the young wizard said slowly, "how can I be certain that you'll return the Prince's throne to him after you've played your part?"

Vincente met Randal's gaze without flinching. "On my honor—Vespian will rule by dawn, or I will be dead."

Randal looked at the actor for a moment longer, and then nodded. "I'll hold you to that."

"So be it," said Vincente. The actor's face was pale and solemn in the blue-white glow of Randal's cold-flame. "But why should you care who governs Peda?"

"I don't know," Randal replied. "I've scarcely met the Prince . . . but I've seen his city, and it seems to me that no one but a good man could produce such peace and plenty, and such lack of fear. And if I don't help a good man when he needs it, then who will help me?"

"Well spoken," said Vincente. "We are agreed, then."

Randal nodded. "Stand still a minute while I work the spell." Once more, he murmured the words that would create a magical disguise—but this time, the spell was at once harder and easier to cast than it should have been.

There's something here that I'm missing, Randal thought as the red-headed actor took on the dark, irregular features of the Prince. *I wish it wasn't so late and I wasn't so tired.*

"When I give the word," Vincente said after the spell was finished, "I want you to do that ghost-effect we've been working on—and make it as dramatic as you possibly can, because we're going to be walking out in front of Bartolomeo's crossbowmen while they're all looking the other way. Once we're center stage with the Duke, they won't dare shoot for fear of hitting him instead."

"I'm ready," said Randal.

Vincente drew his sword. "Begin."

Again Randal whispered the words of illusion and called on the spells of sound and light. He couldn't see the theatre from here in the secret passage, but he'd worked on the ghost's appearance for almost a month now, always standing out of sight in the wings, with only Vincente's criticisms to guide him. *But I never thought that so much would ride on the performance. First the ghost itself, pale and bloodied, and tall enough for everyone in the theatre to see it. And then the sound . . .*

Outside in the theatre, a low moaning began, first softly, then louder, like the wind in pine trees. *Now start the ghost walking forward . . . and let it seem to speak. . . .* Still working blind, Randal set the phantom's mouth to moving and shaped the moaning of the wind into words.

"Treason . . . revenge!"

Vincente opened the secret door. "Now," he said, and stepped out onto the stage, with Randal and Lys close behind him. Randal forced himself not to look out toward the audience and the horrid, half-transparent ghost that he had spent so much time

117

and trouble in perfecting. Instead, he concentrated on the two men in the center of the stage: Duke Bartolomeo, no longer disguised, and Hernando, still wearing the face of Bartolomeo's henchman Carvelli.

Both men stood looking out toward Randal's illusory ghost. "Traitor! Usurper!" the apparition moaned again as Vincente, sword in hand, paced softly to within a few feet of the Duke. Then the actor made a brief cutting gesture with his free hand, and Randal made the phantom disappear.

Vincente took one more step forward.

"How now, brother," the actor said into the sudden, echoing silence, "do you think you are grown so great that you can sit on my throne and rule my lands?"

Bartolomeo turned. If he felt any shock at seeing what appeared to be Vespian still alive and whole, he hid it well. "I thought you were dead," he said. "I see now that I was wrong. But that's a minor problem, and easily corrected."

He drew his own sword.

Randal heard a commotion out in the theatre, and then a man pushed his way through the audience and ran up the steps at the side of the stage. It was the real Carvelli—*I'd almost forgotten about him,* Randal thought; *that was foolish*—and the hedge-magician's features were contorted with anger.

"You have a fellow at your side who wears my face," he called out to Bartolomeo. "Kill him—he is our enemy!"

118

"The man lies," said Hernando coolly. "*He* is the imposter. Shall I kill him for you, Your Grace?"

"As you will, Carvelli," said the Duke. "Settle it between yourselves. My business is with the Prince." Bartolomeo had not taken his eyes off Vincente. Now he smiled. "What do you say, brother: Shall we see which of us is the better man—sword against sword, and winner take all?"

"You leave me no choice," said Vincente. Without looking away from Bartolomeo, the actor said to Randal, "Whatever happens, wizard—hold your hand. This is my fight, not yours."

"Fair enough," said Bartolomeo with a harsh laugh. He turned and called to the guards in the theatre, "This is single combat—you take your orders from the winner."

A few feet away, Hernando and Carvelli already stood facing each other over drawn swords. Now Bartolomeo and Vincente also took positions opposite one another with their swords at the ready. For a moment, nobody moved.

Then Hernando stamped his foot, straightened his arm, and lunged at Carvelli. The hedge-wizard swept the spy's blade aside with his own, so that the point missed his body, and thrust with his own sword toward Hernando. Too late—Hernando had already stepped back out of range.

Lys tugged at the sleeve of Randal's robe, pulling him back upstage, out of the way of the fighting. Randal followed slowly, watching the duelists as he went—in spite of himself, he was fascinated by the unfamiliar style of swordwork. To an onlooker accustomed to the heavy broadswords and thick armor of the northern countries, the combat looked more like a dance than like a fight to the death. The four men in the center of the stage were weaving in a complex pattern: thrusting, parrying, cutting, lunging, charging, and withdrawing, their narrow blades moving so fast the tips could not be seen.

I'd better get a shock-spell ready, thought Randal. *Just in case the wrong man wins and Lys and I have to fight our way out of here.*

The fight continued, the four men moving gracefully amid the sound of steel blades clashing together. Then, as Randal watched, Carvelli stepped back a pace and gestured with his free hand. The grip of Hernando's sword began to glow—first dull red, and then bright.

Carvelli's heating the metal! thought Randal. He'd used the trick once himself, in a pinch, to disarm an opponent bent on killing him.

A smell of scorched flesh wafted over the stage, but Hernando didn't drop the sword. Instead, he lunged. The point of the spy's weapon touched Carvelli's chest and slid on home, penetrating so smoothly that it barely depressed the cloth of the hedge-wizard's tunic. Hernando snapped back into guard, still holding his blade before him—and now fresh blood stained the red-hot metal.

Carvelli looked surprised. Then his sword fell from nerveless fingers to clatter onto the floor of the stage. A moment later, Carvelli toppled, joining his blade. Only then did Hernando let go of his own sword.

The death of Carvelli seemed to propel Bartolomeo and Vincente to even more furious movement. Back and forth they fought. Then the man closer to the front of the stage—Bartolomeo—reached back into his pocket with his left hand. In one smooth movement Bartolomeo snapped his arm forward, and a handful of gold coins flew into Vincente's eyes.

The actor flinched back, his eyes involuntarily shutting, as Bartolomeo followed up his advantage with a deadly lunge. But Vincente must have anticipated the attack. He sidestepped, and the blade passed by, slashing through the black velvet of his tunic. Red blood stained the white linen beneath.

But Bartolomeo's lunge had carried him too far forward, and now he was unable to draw back to guard in time. Vincente, his eyes once more open, drew his blade in a large circle, binding Bartolomeo's weapon. Then he stepped forward—pressing Bartolomeo, tightening the circle of his blade. A final motion of the actor's wrist, and the blade tore from Bartolomeo's hand and flew across the stage. Bartolomeo sank to his knees, Vincente's point at the hollow of his throat.

For a long moment, nobody moved. Finally Vincente drew back his sword. "I should kill you," the actor said to the kneeling Duke. "But we are of the same blood, after all. Go back to your villa, and trouble me no more."

Then Vincente turned away from Bartolomeo and stepped back upstage toward where Lys and Randal still stood watching. "My friends, I must tell you—"

Behind the disguised actor, Bartólomeo rose to his feet—swiftly, silently, drawing a knife from his boot as he came. Before Randal's horrified gaze he started forward, knife at the ready, and all his attention focused on the center of Vincente's back.

X.

The Gratitude of Princes

FOR RANDAL, THE piece of steel in the Duke's hand appeared to be moving with almost infinite slowness. But nobody else on the stage, or in the crowded theatre, seemed to see it at all. Carvelli lay dead, and Hernando stood cradling his burned hand against his chest, gazing down at the hedge-wizard's body. Lys had looked toward Vincente as soon as the actor turned away from his vanquished adversary. Vincente himself had his back to the glittering blade.

Everything was moving so slowly, like falling in a nightmare. But Randal was all too aware that he was awake.

Bartolomeo lunged forward. Nothing could stop the motion that threatened to drive the dagger into Vincente's body.

*I have to knock him aside somehow, and there's no time—*Randal lifted his hand and cast the shock-spell. The magical blow that he had made ready at the fight's beginning ripped free from his mind and struck Bartolomeo full in the chest.

The young wizard watched, his empty hand still upraised. *Too hard. I hit him too hard,* he thought in despair, as the force of the spell toppled Vespian's brother and sent him flying backward off the stage, down into the Prince's high, carved wood throne.

There was a sharp crack as he hit. Randal saw Duke Bartolomeo sitting in the throne where he had fallen, the throne he had tried to steal. The Duke's head was tilted against the back of the heavy chair at an unnatural angle. The edge had taken him squarely in the neck and broken it.

He's dead, Randal thought numbly. *I only wanted to stop him, but he's dead just the same.*

Vincente spun around. The disguised actor strode to the foot of the stage and stood for a long moment looking down at the dead form so similar to the one he now wore. He lifted his head and called out in a tight, controlled voice to the audience and the guards, "Leave us! Leave us, all of you!"

The people left. Vincente did not look away from the theatre until all the benches were empty. Then he turned, and Randal saw that the actor's borrowed features were pale and stiff with anger.

"How dare you?" Vincente demanded. "How *dare* you strike him down after I forbade it?"

Randal felt his own anger rising in response. He flung out his arm and pointed at Bartolomeo's dagger where it had fallen onto the boards of the stage. "That's why," he said. "The Duke was about to stab you in the back. And as for forbidding anything— you're no more the real Prince than I am, and I think you've forgotten the promise you made to me."

The young wizard spoke the words that ended illusion. The spy Hernando once more had his own features, and not those of the dead Carvelli, while Vincente's disguise as Prince Vespian faded away and left the red-headed actor behind.

Then a deep voice spoke from the theatre, out beyond the stage. "Acting hastily and speaking hastily are the two great errors—especially for a wizard. Let all of reality be seen, and then we can determine truth."

The voice belonged to Petrucio. The master wizard—still pale from his near-fatal wound, but healed—came up the steps at the side of the stage and lifted one hand. As he spoke, Randal felt the snapping sensation of a powerful spell breaking. Behind him, he heard Lys gasp.

Vincente no longer was Vincente. All trace of the popular actor had disappeared with the breaking of that last illusion. The man who stood before Randal was Vespian the Magnificent, Prince of Peda.

Randal lowered the hand that still pointed to Bartolomeo's dagger. There was nothing he could think of to say to change what he had already said, nothing he could think of to do—no, that was wrong. There was one thing left to do. He went down on one knee before the Prince.

"I submit myself to Your Grace's justice," he said.

He knelt there without looking up for what seemed like a long time.

Finally the Prince spoke. "Go to your chambers, and remain until you are sent for."

Randal stood, bowed without meeting the Prince's

eyes, turned, and walked away, forcing himself not to run. He made his way through the hallways of the palace like someone in a daze, arriving at his room more by luck than by conscious effort. He threw himself across the bed, still fully dressed.

He couldn't sleep. Instead, he lay with his face buried in his arms, trying to blot out the image of Duke Bartolomeo sprawling limp and lifeless in the Prince's carved wood throne. *I didn't mean to kill him. I only wanted to stop him—is it my fault that he lost his balance and fell?*

But his wizard's training wouldn't let him lie, even to himself. *If I hadn't thrown that shock-spell at Bartolomeo, he wouldn't have died.*

His memories changed and shifted. Instead of Bartolomeo, he saw Nicolas Wariner lying dead in a narrow street in Widsegard. *My fault, too. If I hadn't asked Nick for help—If I hadn't been so quick to get myself involved in stronger magic than I could handle—then he'd still be alive.*

Randal groaned aloud and for a moment wished he could forswear magic entirely, even the tricks and illusions he'd used in the Prince's theatre. But he hadn't been able to do that before, not even when grief over Nick's death was still fresh in his mind; he knew that he could no more abandon wizardry than he could leave off breathing.

Nick couldn't either, he realized. *He tried to find a life for himself outside the Art—but in the end he made his choice and died as a wizard. I'll always feel responsible for his death, but he wouldn't want that to stop me from using my own power when it's needed.*

128

Then another thought came, even more tempting than the idea of quitting wizardry had been. *I could use my power now, to leave the palace. Lys would come with me, and Petrucio wouldn't stop me.*

But when I left Doun to study magic, I made the decision to accept the consequences of my actions. I put myself under the Prince's justice, and that means abiding by his sentence, whatever it might be.

At last, Randal dropped into fitful, exhausted sleep, only to dream all night of trials and punishments, of axe and noose and flame.

❧   ❧   ❧

The next morning, Petrucio himself came to Randal's chamber at first light. The master wizard entered the room without knocking, as if the locking-spells had been nothing more than chains of paper. He carried a large tray with him, and the scent of good food leaked out from under the silver lids of the covered dishes.

"Rise up, young Randal," said Petrucio, setting the tray down on the room's only table. "You have a long road ahead of you, and a good breakfast is always the best start."

Randal struggled out of the last moments of a troubled nightmare and sat up amid the tangled bedcovers. "So it's banishment, then," he said. He was still too weary to feel anything more than a kind of dull relief.

"In a manner of speaking," said Petrucio. The master wizard piled eggs and bread and strips of thick bacon onto a dish and held it out to Randal. "It is not, in fact, His Grace's intent to punish you, in spite of what you seem to fear. I was able to convince him that the Duke's death was an accident, and that you did the best you could under trying circumstances. No one could ask more, and no harm will come to you because of it."

Randal nodded without speaking. After he had finished the plateful of food, he felt somewhat less worn out in body and mind and experienced the first real stirrings of curiosity.

"If the Prince isn't going to punish me," he asked, "then why do I have to leave?"

Petrucio smiled kindly. "I could say that as a journeyman, you belong on the road . . . but that would be considerably less than the whole truth. The fact of the matter is that His Grace can't afford to let you stay in Peda, now that you know his secret."

"That he's Vincente?" Randal picked up a scrap of bread and frowned at it as he crumbled it into his plate. "But if the Prince is Vincente, then who was the man Bartolomeo had in prison at his villa?"

"Perhaps you'd better tell me all your adventures," said the master wizard. "I may be better able to explain things to you once I know everything that happened."

Randal told him about the events of the day before. When he had finished, Petrucio nodded. "Now many things are clearer to me than they were. The Duke's plans were more subtle than usual—if you hadn't spotted Carvelli on his way back from searching your room, we might not have known until too late. But even yesterday, I didn't think everything would start happening so soon—so when

Hernando brought me word that the Duke was expecting a stranger from outside Peda, I took a chance on sending you out fishing for information. I tried to set up a meeting with you after your return, through your friend Lys—but events moved too swiftly for us."

"That still doesn't explain who the third Vincente was," protested Randal. "One was Bartolomeo, whom I disguised. The second was Vespian, and that was your doing. But who was the man I found in the Duke's villa?"

"Ah, yes," said Petrucio. "Vincente. Like Hernando, he works for me. Vincente is kind enough to allow his name and appearance to be borrowed, as it were, by the Prince during the hours His Grace spends with the actors."

Randal thought for a moment. "Then the Vincente I worked with all that time in the theatre—"

"—was really the Prince," finished Petrucio. "Yes. I don't believe you met Vincente himself more than three times—once on that first day in the market square, once in Bartolomeo's prison cell, and once when you healed him. You did an excellent job there, by the way; when I visited my workroom earlier this morning, I found him well on the road to recovery."

"That's good," said Randal. He pushed his empty plate aside. The journeyman's robe he'd fallen asleep in the night before swirled down around his calves as he stood up. He began gathering together his few possessions—clothing mostly, all of it new since he'd come to live in the palace. "If I'm leaving

Peda this morning, does His Grace have any particular place in mind for me to go?"

"As a matter of fact, yes," said Petrucio. He smiled a little. "You know that the Prince lends money, from time to time, to the dukes and earls of Brecelande."

"I know," said Randal. "Vincente—I mean, Prince Vespian—told me as much one day in the theatre."

Petrucio nodded. "Good. An envoy from one of your northern barons is leaving this morning with gold borrowed to pay for a military campaign. As it happens, Vespian's paymaster has been complaining that the envoy's own fighting-men can't provide enough protection. The presence of a wizard with your abilities ought to settle his stomach a little."

Randal gave a short laugh. "So His Grace gets rid of me and finds a guard for his pack train, both at the same time."

"It's a position of considerable trust," said Petrucio gently. "The Prince asks that you stay with the campaign until all the gold has been paid out, to keep the paymaster's courage equal to his task—but once you leave Peda, there's nothing holding you to it except your own word."

"I'll watch his gold for him," said Randal with a sigh. He put the last of his clothing onto the bed and tied the whole thing into a bundle with a spare belt. "What happens to Lys?"

"She travels with you," said Petrucio. "She knows Vespian's secret as well, you see."

Randal picked up his bundle of clothing and slung it over one shoulder. "Then I might as well be off," he said. "Where do I find this envoy?"

132

"I'll show you the way," said Petrucio. They left the room together and proceeded through the quiet, unawakened corridors. As they walked, the master wizard said, "I'll be sorry to lose your assistance, young Randal. Looking into the future has never been the strongest of my talents, but I can see that you have a promising career ahead of you."

If I survive that long, Randal added mentally. The thought called another question to mind. "What happened to the real Master Edmond?" he asked aloud.

"Hernando dealt with him yesterday morning," said Petrucio. "Rather permanently, I suspect. It doesn't pay, I've found, to look too closely into Hernando's methods."

They came out of the palace into a large courtyard near one of the rear gates. A dozen heavily laden pack mules waited there, along with a score of foot soldiers armed in mail and leather after the northern fashion. One of the palace grooms held the bridles of three riding horses, and a second groom devoted his energy to restraining a high-spirited warhorse—a big, heavily muscled animal bred to carry the armored knights of Brecelande into battle.

Randal looked around for Lys and spotted her standing near the groom who held the smaller horses. Once again she was dressed in the boy's garb she wore on the road. A new lute was slung over her shoulder in a leather case. That was good, Randal reflected. Lys's old lute had been lost back in Widsegard, and though she'd never complained, he knew she'd missed the instrument sorely.

"Well," she said to Randal as he joined her, "we're on the road again. And back to Brecelande at that."

"I'm sorry we aren't staying longer in Peda," he replied. Lys's words had sounded cheerful enough, but he still couldn't help feeling guilty about their sudden departure. "I know that Occitania's your home—it can't be easy for you to leave it again so soon."

She shook her head. "I'll miss it, that's true. But I meant what I said that day during rehearsal, about staying as long as you did and no longer. There's something waiting for us in Brecelande that's been left unfinished. If we're going back now, it's because it's time."

As she spoke, a small man dressed after the local fashion came into the courtyard from one of the side entrances. He was complaining loudly to the taller man who paced along beside him. The second man wore the armor and surcoat of a knight of Brecelande. For a moment Randal stared at him in disbelief. Then he let out a yell that echoed off the palace walls.

"Walter!" he shouted. The knight halted and stared in turn. Then he, too, gave a shout.

"Randy!"

The knight strode forward, and Randal found himself caught up in his cousin's mail-clad, back-pounding embrace. Then Walter stepped back, laughing, and held Randal at arms' length.

"So you're the wizard the Prince's man kept going on about," Walter said. "The last time I saw you, it looked like you were heading toward Cingestoun. What on earth are you doing here in Peda?"

"Leaving town in a hurry, as usual," said Lys, coming up from behind Randal.

Walter's broad smile grew even broader. "Demoiselle Lys, as I live and breathe! Still trying to keep my cousin out of trouble, I see."

"And failing," said Lys, with a smile of her own. "We've had some adventures, let me tell you, since you left us to go off questing in the Western Isles."

Randal gave his cousin a curious glance. "How did that go, anyway? Stories I've heard about the Isles talk of everything from pirates to sea-dragons, with mermaids in between."

"It's all true," Walter assured him. "I had enough trouble on that quest to last me the rest of my days— I give you my word, I'd sooner it had happened to someone else, especially the parts where I was seasick."

"So what are you doing here?" asked Randal, laughing.

Walter looked a bit sheepish. "Word about my adventures got back home to Brecelande," he admitted. "So when the baron needed his gold fetched northward from Peda, people said, 'Why not send a hero to guard the gold?'" The knight shrugged. "Since I didn't have anything else to do, here I am."

"You've sworn fealty to this baron, then?" Randal inquired.

"Only that I'd see his money delivered and kept safe," said Walter. "Nothing more. And he's an honorable man, by all accounts, so I saw nothing wrong with the plan. The trip's been easy enough so far." He paused a moment. "You don't have any premonitions about it, do you?"

"No," said Randal. "Any bad dreams I've had lately have been strictly my own."

"Well, I'm grateful for your company just the same," said Walter. "And I won't deny that a wizard's help might come in handy along the way. Let's mount up and be off—I want to be out of the city by full daylight."

Randal turned to bid farewell to Master Petrucio, but the wizard had gone. The party mounted their horses—Randal, Lys, and Vespian's paymaster on the smaller palfreys and Walter on the charger. Walter gave a command to his troop, and the pack train moved out through the palace gates.

The streets of Peda were still empty as Randal and the others made their way through the town and into the countryside. The close-packed houses gave way to cottages and small gardens, and then to the open road.

As the pack train went on past fields of grazing cattle, Randal became aware of hoofbeats on the road behind them, the noise loud in the morning stillness. He looked over his shoulder and saw a single rider on a black horse, coming up fast. The early sunlight caught on the rider's bright red hair.

"I think I know who this is," said Randal quietly to Walter. "I'll talk to him." He turned his horse and headed back past the tail of the pack train to meet the oncoming rider and speak with him alone.

As Randal had expected, it was Vincente. The actor looked tired, as if he hadn't slept at all between midnight and this morning. Randal quietly cast the spell of magical resonance as the actor drew closer, and nodded to himself as the echo of powerful magic came back at him. *I thought so. But if he wants to speak as Vincente, and not as the Prince, I'll give him the chance.*

"What brings you out of the palace so early?" he asked, as Vincente reined his horse to a halt.

"An errand for His Grace," said Vincente. "He wishes to apologize for hustling you out of town so abruptly . . . and if I'm not mistaken, for words spoken in anger as well."

"There's no need," said Randal. "He had reason enough, I think, to be angry with me."

Vincente was silent for a minute, while the black horse moved restlessly beneath him. "That may be so," he said finally. "But he's in your debt for his life and wouldn't have you leave thinking him ungrateful." The red-headed actor reached into a pocket of his tunic and drew out a black velvet bag. He handed it to Randal. "His Grace desires you to have this, as some small repayment."

Randal took the bag and hefted it in the palm of his hand. Coins rolled and shifted inside the black velvet—gold, from the weight and sound of them. He held the bag for a minute, and then handed it back to Vincente with a shake of his head.

"I can make my way without it," he said. "Tell His Grace for me that I don't need his money . . . and I would much rather have his friendship than his gratitude."

Vincente took the bag of coins and tucked it into his pocket. "Princes deal in gold, not gratitude," he said, with a rather melancholy expression, "and they can't afford friendship. But an actor sometimes can."

He held out his hand again, and this time it was empty. "You'll be missed, Randal—it's a pity we never got a chance to present that ghost of yours properly."

Randal laughed and clasped the outstretched hand with his own scarred one. "I'd call it a success just the same," he said. "Goodbye, Vincente."

"Goodbye, and good luck." The actor turned and spurred his horse toward the city. Randal sat for a while watching him, and then rode back to join Walter and Lys at the head of the pack train.

"Who was that man?" asked his cousin.

"Nobody you'd recognize," said Randal. "Only a friend, saying goodbye."

He looked back again at the road behind them, but Vincente was gone. Randal sighed, straightened his shoulders, and rode on away from Peda, toward Brecelande and home.